Don Harding had taken on a dirty fight . . .

with the same kind of vicious meanness in it
that had killed his brother. And because everyone had something to hide, everyone's hand
was against him. So he didn't know where the
next attack would come from.

Harding went out and bought a headstone for
his brother's grave:

SAMMY HARDING—born 1856, died 1876
Lynched by a bunch of cowards
for a crime he did not commit.

And just to make sure the town understood his
intentions, Don put up another headstone. The
name and date were blank, but the sentiments
were clear:

• •
Executed by Don Harding
for the murder of his brother.

Other Books by Edwin Booth

Outlaw Town
Reluctant Lawman

SIDEWINDER
Edwin Booth

WILDSIDE PRESS

CHAPTER ONE

AT A FORK in the trail, someone had put up a crude sign, "PARADISE—3 miles," with an arrow pointing to the right. Across it, a disgruntled traveller had scrawled, "A damn lie."

Don Harding sat his dusty sorrel and smiled in appreciation of the unknown critic's postscript. He, too, was dubious about there being anything closely approximating paradise in this sun-baked corner of Arizona. Also, he was acquainted with the popular custom of naming a town for what someone hoped it would turn into, rather than for what it was, so that a place called Cold Springs was as likely as not to be only a dried-up buffalo wallow, and New Boston was just a lonely adobe saloon in the middle of nowhere.

Nevertheless, the sign took some of the slump out of his shoulders, since it meant that after two weeks in the saddle he was almost home. Home, that was, if he could apply the term to a place he had never seen, and which he knew about only through his brother's brief and infrequent letters.

Thinking of Sammy erased the smile from his face, and prompted him to stir the sorrel into motion. It had been three months since the last letter, and he couldn't help being a little worried. For that matter, most of his life he had been worried about Sammy, at least since their folks had died thirteen years before, when he had been seventeen, and Sammy only seven. Of course, now that they had this ranch, those worries would presumably end.

As so often happens, the last few miles seemed twice as long as any that had gone before. However, at the age of thirty, Don Harding had finally learned to temper impatience with self-control, so he let the tired sorrel pick its own slow pace. Meanwhile he occupied his time by sizing up the country through which he was riding.

The ranch, according to Sammy's directions, would be located on the other side of the town of Paradise, but the terrain would probably be similar to this: gently rolling prairie, too dry to support any worthwhile vegetation, with genuine desert not far to the south, and a low line of tree-covered hills about the same distance to the north. Of course, the ranch would differ from this in one respect, since there was a creek running across it, its water nourishing the grazing land which would feed his and Sammy's cows.

The town of Paradise, when it finally came into view, proved to be more pretentious than Don had anticipated. Its single business block, in addition to the inevitable saloon, general store, and livery stable, also boasted a bank, a hotel with a wooden awning, and a restaurant, as well as several other business establishments not readily identifiable from a distance.

Scattered haphazardly around the business section were two or three dozen houses of various shapes and sizes. The biggest of these, in fact the only one which was two stories high, had dark red curtains at all its windows. As though this were not enough of a hint to its nature, a pair of ruffled pink pantaloons hung limply from a stick fastened to the chimney.

This made Don chuckle, but he didn't waste time speculating as to how the unusual pennant chanced to be there. There were more important things on his mind, the first of these being to learn the exact location of the ranch.

The sorrel slowed down hopefully in front of the livery stable, but, when Don lifted the reins half an inch, it went on, not stopping again until he headed it in at the hitchrail outside the Dancing Lady Saloon.

As he swung down from his saddle and took a twist of the leathers around the hitchrail, Don let his gaze move along the street. Besides the establishments he had noted from the edge of town, there was a saddle shop, a pharmacy, and a small office above whose door was a sign reading "SHERIFF."

Just beyond the sheriff's office was another sign which said, "NICK'S CAFE, N. Napoleon, Prop." As Don stepped onto the wooden sidewalk, unconsciously reaching down to loosen the pistol in his holster, he had a fleeting glimpse of a girl looking at him through the cafe's window. Since he was not interested in girls at the moment, either the kind who would work in a cafe or those in the big house with the red curtains, he gave it no further thought. Pushing open the saloon's batwing doors, he went in.

The interior was dark compared to the sunlight outside, and for a moment Don couldn't see too clearly. Habit made him move aside from the opening, and when he realized what he had done, he shook his head in exasperation. How long would it be, he wondered, before he broke himself of expecting trouble where none existed?

There were two customers in the place, and a bartender. One of the customers was a smallish man in town clothes. The other was as big as Don, or at any rate a good six feet tall, and was wearing a brass star on his vest. Both men had turned toward the door, and were watching with interest.

The room smelled strongly of spilled beer, reminding Don that he hadn't had so much as a sip of water since breakfast. However, before satisfying his thirst, he wanted to find out about Sammy. He crossed the room and nodded to the man with the badge.

"Likely you're the man I was hoping to find, Sheriff. Can you tell me how to get to the H Bar H?"

"H Bar H?" The sheriff frowned, and shook his head. "You're on the wrong range, mister; ain't no place of that name around here."

There was a thinly veiled arrogance in the sheriff's tone, as though he were daring anyone to challenge his statement. Don had encountered this attitude before, usually in dealing with men who had attained positions giving them a small amount of authority, and had let it go to their heads. However, he didn't intend to make an issue of it, so he said mildly:

"Maybe I'm mistaken about the name of the ranch, but

I'm certain who's running it, because he's my brother. His name is Harding—Sammy Harding."

An exploding bomb couldn't have made a more pronounced effect on the three men. The bartender dropped the glass he had been drying and it shattered on the polished counter; the little man in store clothes gasped an astounded, "Gawdamighty!" and the sheriff's eyes widened in amazement.

"You're telling me that you're Sammy Harding's brother?"

Don nodded, realizing that something was wrong, but not yet able to guess what it was. When no one offered to explain, he said bluntly, "Now that you know who I am, maybe you'll tell me where I can find my brother."

The sheriff's eyes had recovered their normal size, and his thick lips twisted into what might have passed for a grin.

"Sure, mister; I'll tell you where you can find Sammy Harding. Matter of fact, I'll show you. Come over to the door."

Don slanted a quick look at the other two, saw that they were watching him as though hypnotized, and turned to follow the sheriff, who pushed open the batwings and stepped out onto the sidewalk.

"There's where you'll find him, mister, right up on that hill." He pointed.

Don looked where the sheriff was pointing, and his blood turned cold at the sight of the wooden crosses.

"You mean Sammy's dead? Who killed him?"

The sheriff lifted his heavy shoulders in a shrug.

"That's hard to say. Was it the man that tied the rope around his neck, or the one that whipped his horse out from under him? Or was it the other fifteen or twenty that dragged him out of his shack?"

"My God! You mean he was lynched? But what for? Sammy didn't go around making trouble for anyone. He wouldn't step on a bug if he could help it. No one would have reason to . . ."

"Suppose you try telling that to Cletus Culver," the sheriff said. "After all, it was his daughter your brother raped, not mine."

CHAPTER TWO

DON HARDING WAS not usually an easy man to surprise, but for a moment after the sheriff quit talking, he was too stunned to answer. Not so much at the announcement that Sammy was dead, as at the way in which it had happened. Death was one of the things you learned to expect in this uncivilized country, but not at the hands of a mob, for an offense such as the sheriff had so bluntly specified. Especially not to a boy like Sammy, who had inherited many of the gentle characteristics of their mother. For years, most of Don's worries about his brother had stemmed from his fear that the boy would be taken advantage of on account of his mild nature. For anyone to accuse Sammy of a crime like this was unthinkable.

Not only unthinkable, it wasn't true. Don tore his gaze away from the graveyard, and looked squarely into the sheriff's eyes.

"The thing you just said about my brother—it's a lie. Now tell me what really happened."

"Why damn you!" the sheriff exploded. "No one can call Yank Yankton a liar and get away . . ."

His hand clawed at his gun, but before it could clear leather, Don had drawn his own pistol and brought the barrel down across the sheriff's wrist, making him grunt with pain.

"I'd advise you not to make that mistake twice, Sheriff. Ordinarily, I don't draw a gun without pulling the trigger. Now go on; tell me the truth about my brother."

The sheriff's face was almost purple with rage as he said sullenly, "It's just like I already told you, mister. Your brother was stringing bobwire between his place and Cul-

9

ver's Box C. Minnie Culver came riding by, just meaning to
be neighborly, and . . ." He raised his eyebrows suggestively.

The batwing doors of the saloon inched open and the
little man who had been talking to the sheriff squeezed between them, edged cautiously along the front of the building, and took off across the street at an angle, picking up
speed as he approached the livery stable at the far end of
the block. Don noted all this without taking his eyes off
the sheriff.

"I suppose you're going to tell me that Sammy pulled the
girl off her horse and tore the clothes off her. Is that the general idea?" He shook his head in disbelief. "Even if it
wasn't my brother we were talking about, if it was some
half-breed just out of Yuma Prison, I wouldn't swallow a
yarn like that. Not unless the girl was simple-minded. If
she wasn't, she'd have sense enough not to get that close to
someone she didn't know."

The sheriff looked down at his wrist, which was beginning
to swell, then up at Don.

"She got close enough, all right, one way or another. If
you won't take my word for it, ask Doc White."

It was becoming apparent that there was little to be
learned by talking to the sheriff. Also, word of what was
happening had evidently spread along the street, for two
or three doors had been opened. As Don diverted his attention from the sheriff long enough to glance toward the townsmen who had come out onto the sidewalk to stare across at
the saloon, a horseman rode out of the livery stable and took
off toward the west, looking back over his shoulder until he
was out of sight. Don turned back to the sheriff.

"We'll go into this again, Sheriff. Right now, I've got just
one more question. When they lynched my brother, what
did you do to stop them?"

Without waiting for an answer, Don deliberately turned
his back and stepped down into the dust of the street. He
was fully aware that the sheriff would like nothing better
than to put a bullet in his back, but he didn't think it was
liable to happen in front of so many people. Without another
glance at the sheriff, he untied his horse, swung into the saddle, and headed toward the livery stable.

At first the big barn seemed empty. Then a door at the

back opened, and a lanky, stoop-shouldered man came into sight. He squinted at Don a moment, then moved closer and said, "Something I can do for you, Mr. Harding?"

Don frowned at the use of his name, and the man nodded toward the room he had just come out of.

"Seth Huddleson told me who you were. He's back there now, waiting for you to leave." He grinned. "After seeing you handle the sheriff, he's in no hurry to get better acquainted."

Don looked at the closed door, and recalled something the sheriff had said. Was Huddleson the one who had placed the noose around Sammy's neck? Or could it have been this hostler? He stepped out of the saddle, and handed over the reins.

"Wait until I untie this warbag, then you can strip him down and put him in a clean stall. He's come a long way, so don't be stingy with the grain. I'll be back."

"Yes sir," the liveryman said, his grin broadening. "Anything else, General?"

Don studied him a moment, and said mildly, "Why yes, I guess there is. Can you tell me where I'd be likely to find Doc White?"

"In his office, I reckon. It's the last building on this side of the block. Doc's office is in the back."

"Thanks." Don tucked the warbag under his left arm, and went out onto the street.

Only half an hour had elapsed since he had ridden into the town of Paradise, but already the atmosphere had changed. Then, it had been just another town; now, there was a feeling of tension in the air. Men faded unobtrusively out of sight into the stores as he walked toward Doc White's office. By the time he had passed a vacant lot next to the livery and reached the front of the hotel, the street was deserted.

He smiled grimly and continued on his way, his boots rattling the wooden sidewalk. He passed the bank, then another vacant lot, and turned in at the pharmacy. A short, sandy-haired man was about to come out the door, and, on a hunch, Don said, "Dr. White?"

"That's me, son. From what Sheriff Yankton just told

me, I reckon you must be Harding, although that isn't the
only name he called you. What's on your mind?"

Don looked around inside the pharmacy without seeing
anyone. He focused his attention on the doctor.

"If you've been talking to the sheriff, you probably know
why I'm here. What can you tell me about a girl named
Minnie Culver?"

"I could tell you a lot of things, young man, but I doubt
if you'd be interested. If you want to know whether she's
carrying a baby, the answer is yes. Ordinarily, that'd be nobody's business except hers and mine, but it looks like
this time it's everyone's, so you might as well know that
she's about four months along. Is that all you wanted to find
out?"

"Unless you can tell me who the father is."

"If I could do that," the doctor said, "I wouldn't be
wasting my time in a place like Paradise. Now if you're
done, I've got some calls to make."

Don stepped outside, and watched until the doctor had
reached the livery stable and gone in, then he retraced his
steps to the shade of the hotel awning. He hadn't planned on
staying in Paradise overnight, but the way things had
turned out, there was no point leaving town in a hurry. Certainly there was no inducement to reach the ranch, now
that Sammy would not be there to greet him. He opened
the hotel door and went in.

The hotel lobby was a big uncarpeted room with several
straightback chairs, a counter diagonally across one corner,
and an unrailed flight of stairs leading to the upper floor.
Behind the desk was the little man who had been in the
saloon, the one the liveryman had called Seth Huddleson.
Apparently he had come in through a back door, as Don
hadn't seen him on the street. He had the look of a man
who would use back doors.

Huddleson was watching Don uneasily, looking as though
he were tempted to make a run for it. He backed away
from the counter as Don moved up, put down his warbag,
and said, "I'll be staying here tonight. Maybe longer, depending on how things work out. Shall I pay you now, or
when I leave?"

The little man swallowed painfully, and shook his head.

"Afraid you're out of luck, mister. We're full up."

Surprised, Don looked at Huddleson sharply. The little man dropped his eyes, and Don glanced past him at a dozen or so keys hanging from nails driven into a board which was hung against the wall. It was obvious that the man was lying. Instead of telling him so, Don leaned across the counter and lifted the whole keyrack off its hook.

"One of these ought to fill the bill," he said pleasantly. "I'll bring the others back when I come down."

"Hey!" Huddleson protested. "You can't do that. You've got no business . . ."

"And you won't have," Don cut in, "if you treat all your customers the way you're treating me." He picked up his warbag and went up the stairs, leaving Huddleson muttering to himself. Half an hour later, having chosen a room overlooking the street, and washed away some of the dust of the trail, he returned to the lobby and laid the keyrack in front of the hotelman.

"I'll be staying in number six, in case anyone's looking for me." He dug a silver dollar out of his pocket and dropped it on the counter. "This ought to cover the first night. If I decide to stay longer, we'll work it out."

Huddleson had apparently been nursing his resentment, and fortifying himself as well, for he said with a show of spirit, "If you're smart, mister, you won't be staying longer than one night. You ain't going to be popular around here."

"I'm not sure I'd like to be popular in a town like this," Don said, and went out onto the sidewalk.

A brief inspection of the street disclosed nothing different except the changed angles of the shadows made by the declining sun. It seemed as thought the citizens of Paradise were reluctant to show themselves in the open. Ashamed, most likely, because of the part they had played in the lynching. Don stepped down into the road and headed across toward the cafe, not that he was especially hungry, but because it had been a long time since breakfast, and there was no sense starving himself over circumstances which he couldn't help.

It was an off hour, and there were no diners in the cafe. Don chose a table where he could sit with his back to a wall, and glanced toward the doorway to the kitchen. It occurred to him that he might meet the same reception here that he had received at the hotel. A little flicker of anger tightened his jaw muscles, then he recognized the humor of the situation, and grinned. It could get downright aggravating if he had to wait on himself wherever he went. Still, he would do it if necessary. He would even go out in that kitchen and fix his own grub, if someone didn't show up pretty damn quick.

Fortunately, before this became necessary, a girl came out of the back room and moved over beside his table. She was rather nice looking, in a subdued sort of way. Her dark hair was pulled back into a severe knot, and the dress she wore seemed unnecessarily drab. All in all, not a girl who would make men turn for a second look.

"Good afternoon," she said politely, and some quality in her voice caught Don's interest. "You're a little early for our regular supper, but if there's anything else I can get you, I'm at your service."

"Whatever's handiest," Don said. "I'm not fussy about my food, so long as it doesn't poison me."

She smiled, and said pleasantly, "I believe I can promise you *that* much, if you don't mind waiting a few minutes."

Don nodded, and watched her start back toward the kitchen. As she was about to pass through the doorway, he said abruptly, "Before you go any farther, maybe it's only fair to tell you who I am. I'm Sammy Harding's brother."

She looked back at him, her face composed.

"How do you do, Mr. Harding. I'm Helen Sprecher. I suppose you'll want your coffee black?"

Again Don nodded, and she disappeared into the kitchen, leaving him somewhat puzzled. Surely, in a town the size of this, everyone would know what had happened to Sammy, yet she had acted as though it didn't mean a thing.

While he was speculating on it, the sound of horses in the street swung him around to face the window. Two horsemen were pulling up at the hotel hitchrail, one of them, a solidly built man with a fringe of gray hair showing beneath the brim of his hat, the other, a rawboned individual who appeared to be considerably younger. They dismounted and entered the hotel, the younger one stepping aside respectfully to let the other go first.

From the speed at which they had ridden in, Don was
reasonably sure their visit had some connection with his own
arrival in town. Especially since they had come from the
direction taken by the man who had hurried out of the
livery stable shortly after Seth Huddleson had gone in. It
wasn't unreasonable to assume that the older man would be
Cletus Culver, the girl's father. If so, he was probably
questioning the hotelman as to Don's whereabouts.

The hotel door opened again, and the two men came out.
From the way in which they both looked across toward the
cafe, it was apparent that they now knew where Don was.
They started across the street, giving Don his first good
view of their features.

Culver's face looked as though it had been chiseled out of
weather-stained granite. He had a powerful jaw, a promi-
nent nose, and eyes which at the moment were narrowed
to slits. An unlit cigar was clamped between thick lips, and
he gave the impression that if anything got in his way, he'd
walk right through it.

There wasn't much time for a look at his companion, for
Culver crossed the sidewalk in two steps, jerked open the
cafe door, and burst into the room, his eyes immediately
fixing on Don.

"Are you the one that calls himself Harding?"

Before answering, Don deliberately looked beyond Culver
at his companion. He saw a man about his own age and size,
with a face darkened by long exposure to sun and wind, and
a pair of pale blue eyes which returned his scrutiny with
casual curiosity.

"By God, I asked you a question!" Culver said furiously.
"I'm waiting for an answer."

"And I'm waiting for some grub," Don said. "Maybe by
the time I've eaten it, you'll cool off enough to act civil. If
you do, I'll be happy to swap a few questions with you."

"Why you insolent young ..."

"Take it easy, Mr. Culver," the other man said softly.
"There's no use getting upset over this. Besides you
wouldn't want to start anything when there's a lady
present." He nodded toward the kitchen door.

Don thought it might be a ruse to make him turn his head,
but just then the girl came into sight carrying a plate of

food. Without giving any indication that she noticed anything wrong, she set the plate in front of Don, frowned at
it a second as if to make sure she hadn't forgotten anything,
then straightened up and gave the other two a friendly smile.

"Would you gentlemen like some coffee while you wait?
There's plenty in the pot."

Culver glared at her, seemed about to give vent to his
anger, then got control of himself enough to say curtly,
"No thanks. We're not thirsty."

Don couldn't help smiling at the way the girl had handled
the situation. He noticed that Culver's companion was grinning appreciatively, too, yet he had the feeling that, of the
two men, the younger would be the one to watch in case of
trouble.

Culver had evidently decided to heed the other man's advice, but it was obvious that he had no intention of leaving
until he had accomplished his purpose. He stood with his
legs braced apart, fists clenched at his sides while the girl
brought Don's coffee. When she returned to the kitchen,
he said thickly, "All right, so you've showed us how tough
you are. Now, would you mind telling me if your name's
Harding?"

"Since you put it that way," Don told him, "I'll be glad
to. Yes I'm named Harding. I'm Sammy Harding's brother.
Would I be right in assuming that you're Cletus Culver?"

Culver nodded, and Don added quietly, "Then the gentle-
man with you is . . .?"

"Whitey Larson," Culver growled. "My foreman at Box
C."

"All right, now that we all know each other, what did you
want to talk about?"

"Damn it, you've got guts to ask a question like that.
Talking ain't a specialty of mine, but what I've got to say
can be said in four words—get out of town."

"And if I don't?"

"Oh you will," Culver said harshly. "If you're too damned
dumb to go on your own power, there's other ways."

"Like lynching me, I suppose, the way you did my
brother." Don shook his head. "Don't bet on it, Culver. The
folks in this town don't like themselves very much right now,
and it'll take more than free liquor to make them forget

what they did to Sammy. Especially since you can't give them any legitimate reason for getting rid of me."

"You're his brother," Culver growled. "That's reason enough. If you think I'm going to let you hang around, so that people can point you out and say, 'There's the man whose brother...' " Culver grated to a stop.

"If that's all that's worrying you, you can forget it. Sammy had nothing to do with the fix your daughter's in, and, by the time the baby's born, I intend to prove it."

"Then you ain't going to leave?"

"Why should I? I've done nothing to be ashamed of. Neither did Sammy, when the truth's known. Besides, I've got a ranch to run."

"You're a fool!" Culver said with venom. "You won't last six weeks." He shoved his jaw out belligerently. "For that matter, how does anyone know the ranch is really yours? Chances are..."

"Fortunately for me, I have the deed. Sammy sent it to me as soon as the money changed hands. In case you're interested, the property's in my name."

"Supposing it is?" Culver said impatiently. "You still can't make a go of it. Not the way folks around here feel about anyone named Harding. Nobody will work for you, and you'll have no place to buy supplies. Inside of a month, you're going to be so sick of this country you'll wish you'd never heard of it."

"I already am," Don said dryly, "and you're not making me like it any better. Now suppose you go throw your weight around somewhere else for a while. I'd like to eat this food before it gets any colder."

Blood surged into Culver's face, but before he could do anything rash, Whitey Larson stepped in front of him and faced Don across the table.

"You don't scare easy, Harding, I'll grant you that. But guts alone won't get you far. Not with everyone remembering the stunt your brother pulled."

"As to that," Don said. "I'd come nearer believing it if I heard it from the girl herself."

"Why damn you!" Culver rasped, shoving his foreman aside. "You get within a mile of my daughter and I'll kill you!"

Don looked at him a moment, shrugged, and picked up his fork. With a curse, Culver turned and stomped out of the cafe, the foreman following.

CHAPTER THREE

FROM HIS SEAT at the table, Don watched the two men cross the street to where they had tied their horses. Culver yanked his reins loose from the hitchrail and flung himself into the saddle, every gesture indicating a driving fury. Larson went about it more calmly and without wasting effort. When they were both mounted, Culver turned toward the hotel and shouted, "Huddleson!"

The hotel door opened so promptly that it was obvious that Huddleson had been watching from inside. He stepped out onto the walk, darted a look at the cafe, then peered up at Cletus Culver. The rancher said something which Don couldn't hear, waited only long enough for Huddleson to nod that he understood, then whirled his mount away from the rail and took off at a gallop, with Whitey Larson close behind. Huddleson hesitated a moment at the edge of the walk, glanced uneasily across the street, and retreated into the hotel.

From the kitchen doorway, Helen Sprecher said quietly, "I suppose you realize what you've just done, Mr. Harding. It's the first time anyone has talked back to Cletus Culver in years. He'll never forgive you."

"That's pretty much the impression I got myself," Don said. He turned to glance at her, and added quickly, "Are you feeling all right, miss? You look a little peaked."

"Peaked?" She laughed wryly. "I don't know why in the world I should. After all, nothing happened except that I came within a hair of having a shooting spree right under my nose. I suppose that's just part of running a restaurant, like filling the sugar bowls or mopping the floor."

"You sure acted like it while it was happening," Don said. "The way you took the wind out of Culver's sails with that business about the coffee, by golly, I thought he'd bust a blood vessel." He grinned at the recollection.

"That's right, make a big joke of it," she flared, color returning to her cheeks. "You're all alike, you men; the only way you know to settle things is with a gun."

"It wasn't my idea," Don protested. "All I came in for was some food. When your friend Culver busted in and told me to get out of town, what did you expect me to do? kiss his feet like the rest of them?"

"No," she conceded. "I wouldn't have liked that, either." She made a grimace of annoyance. "I've got no business telling you how to run your life. All I ask is that the next time it happens, you make it happen someplace else."

"Meaning you'd rather I didn't come in here any more?"

"That isn't what I said, and you know it. Don't put words in my mouth." She turned abruptly and went into the kitchen.

Don listened to the angry banging of pots and pans, and grinned crookedly. So far, he was doing real well. The only folks he'd had trouble with were the sheriff, Seth Huddleson, Cletus Culver and his foreman, and now this girl. Come to think of it, those were about all he'd had occasion to talk to. And they called the place Paradise!

The girl didn't reappear before Don finished his meal, so he slid a dollar under the plate, and left. Outside, he paused to consider his next move. There was really very little reason to stay in town, but it was too near sundown to start looking for the ranch. Besides, now that Culver had ordered him to leave, he was determined to stay at least one night. He glanced along the street, saw the little graveyard, and turned his steps in that direction.

There were only a couple of dozen graves, most of them badly neglected. A few of the newer ones had wooden markers on which the inscriptions were still legible. None of these bore the name Harding.

For a second, Don's hopes rose. Perhaps Sammy wasn't dead after all. Maybe this was all some kind of trick. Then he saw an unmarked mound of dirt some distance from the others, and realized what had happened. After lynching Sammy, the town had denied him even the dignity of a marker.

Don crossed to the nameless grave, his heart a lump of lead. There was still no proof that the grave was Sammy's, but he didn't doubt that it was. He picked up a handful of the sandy soil and let it trickle through his fingers. If this *was* his brother's, someone was going to pay. He turned, hard-eyed, toward the town, and saw a stranger climbing laboriously up the hill toward him.

The man was old, possibly in his late seventies, and he was helping himself along with a cane. When he reached a spot ten yards away, he stopped and regarded Don curiously while he recovered his breath. Finally, he hawked, spat in the dust, and said querulously, "You lookin' for something, mister? If you are, I'm the feller to talk to."

"This grave," Don said, pointing. "Whose is it?"

The old man moved a few steps closer, studied Don with faded eyes, and said crossly, "Now hold on a minute. Before I answer a question like that, I better know who's askin' it. What's your name?"

"Harding," Don said, and noticed how the old man stiffened. "Quit stalling, old timer, and give me a straight answer."

The old man squinted at him a moment, then nodded grudgingly.

"It's the one you think it is, all right. The feller they . . ." He moistened his lips, and said, "Sammy Harding, that's whose it is."

"Then why isn't there something to say so?"

The old man shook his head, and would have turned away without answering, but Don stepped across the grave and took hold of his shoulder.

"Just a minute, old timer. I asked you a question. Why isn't there a name 'over my brother's grave?"

The old man made a feeble attempt to dislodge Don's hand, gave it up, and said tonelessly, "None of my business, mister. You might ask Cletus Culver; he gives most of the orders around here. Now will you leave me be?"

"Just one more thing. Who made those other markers?"
Don nodded toward the main part of the graveyard.

"Will Tully, the feller that runs the livery barn."

"Much obliged," Don said. He reached into his pocket
for a two-bit piece and pressed it into the old man's hand.
"I'm sorry if I treated you rough. Go buy yourself a drink."

The old man looked at the coin, and licked his lips as
though already savoring what it would buy at the saloon.
He peered up at Don.

"You say your name's Harding, and that it's your brother under the dirt?"

Don nodded.

"In that case..." The old man dropped the quarter on
the ground and hobbled away without another word.

Don frowned at his back for a few seconds, then turned
to face the grave. It wasn't his nature to indulge in melodra-
matics, nor was he a religious man. So he just stood there for
a few minutes, remembering. Then he turned away and went
down the hill.

When Will Tully had listened to what Don wanted him to
do, he looked up at him obliquely.

"Let me get this straight, Mr. Harding. You want it to say
'Sammy Harding—born 1856—lynched 1876 by a bunch
of cowards for a crime he didn't commit.' Is that it?"

"That's it," Don said bluntly. "And I want to pick it up
the first thing tomorrow morning." He took out a leather
pouch and extracted a five dollar bill. "Will this be enough?"

The hostler grinned.

"It's plenty, but while you're about it, you'd be smart to
order half a dozen. I suppose you know how long this'll stay
up?"

Don had already thought of this possibility. He took a
second five out of the pouch and handed it over.

"I want you to make another one. Leave the name and
date blank. Just say: 'Executed by Don Harding for de-
stroying a grave marker.' "

Tully frowned. "You're fixing to put this...?"

"I'm not putting it anywhere—yet. When it's finished, just
leave it in plain sight where everyone that comes in will
see it. I'll be by for the other one in the morning." Without

waiting for Tully to answer, Don left the barn. He paused out in front to roll a cigarette, and stood smoking it until he heard Tully's saw biting into wood. After that, he made his leisurely way to the front of the hotel and took up a position beneath the wooden awning, with his back to the unpainted boards.

By then it was close to six o'clock, and the merchants would normally be getting ready to shut down for the night. So far, none of them had made an appearance except at the time he had had his run-in with the sheriff. He decided to stand right where he was and see what would happen.

Nothing did, except that one or two of the townsmen opened their doors, saw him waiting, and quickly ducked back inside. At seven o'clock he walked past the bank to the pharmacy, and found both places dark. Evidently the proprietors had left by the way of back doors. The same seemed to be true of the General Store and Saddle Shop across the way. Evidently the town of Paradise had decided he was a killer. Grimly amused, Don entered the hotel, crossed the deserted lobby, and climbed the stairs. It was still uncomfortably warn in his room, so he left the door open on the chance of getting a little breeze, stripped to the waist, and moved the room's only chair over beside the window.

Now that he had left the street, a few of the townsmen had ventured into the open. In the course of an hour, three of them entered the Dancing Lady Saloon, and two others went into the cafe, where a lamp was now glowing. Don's vantage point was too high to give him a very good view of the inside of the cafe, but he caught an occasional glimpse of Helen Sprecher as she moved past the window. It crossed his mind that he hadn't seen anything of the proprietor, N. Napoleon.

By nine o'clock, the two men left the cafe and entered the saloon. A litle later the cafe lamp went out. The girl didn't come out onto the street, so Don assumed that she must have living quarters in the rear. At about this same time, Sheriff Yankton came out of his office between the saloon and the cafe. Don saw him momentarily in the light of the doorway, then there was only the red glare of a cigar to indicate his location. This bobbed along past the saloon,

where his head and shoulders were silhouetted for a moment above the batwings, then continued down the street.

Making his evening circuit of the town, Don presumed, recalling how he had done the same thing himself each evening for a year when he had held a job as marshal of a Kansas railhead. He supposed things went on pretty much according to custom everywhere, even in a town which had lynched an innocent boy.

Bitterness filled his heart, and he let his hand fall to his holstered gun. It would be so simple to even the score with bullets, but what would it prove? Not that Sammy was innocent, just that his brother could handle a gun. And where would he start? So far, he didn't know who the ringleaders were. He got to his feet and began pacing back and forth across the room, his thoughts bleak.

After a few minutes, the mood passed, and he returned to the window. A breeze had sprung up, bringing the scent of sage, and by the time the sheriff had completed his rounds and gone back to the office, it was cool enough for Don to close the door. There was no lock, of course, so he braced the chair against it as best he could, pulled off his boots, hung his gunbelt on the bedpost, and lay down without bothering to remove his pants. Ten minutes later, in spite of everything that was on his mind, he fell asleep.

In common with most men who live in close proximity to danger, Don had developed the ability to awaken at the slightest unusual noise. He did so now, and lay perfectly still waiting for the sound to be repeated. When it came, just the faint creak of a dry board, he eased out of bed, lifted his pistol from its holster, and flattened himself against the wall next to the window.

Someone was outside on the wooden awning. Since the moon was now up, bathing the street in light, Don couldn't risk showing his face at the opening, but he heard stealthy movements as the man crawled toward the window. A dark form came into view above the sill, and assumed the shape of a man's head and shoulders.

Don's pistol was lined up for what would surely have been a fatal shot, but he didn't squeeze the trigger. The man on the awning was obviously contemplating an act of violence, but he was probably only a hireling of someone higher up.

Killing him now wouldn't solve much. It would be better to
wait and see what he was up to.

There wasn't much of a wait. The man reached an arm
into the room and tossed something onto the bed. Without
a moment's hesitation, he disappeared from sight. A second
later there was the sound of running footsteps down in the
street.

Don's first thought was that the man had thrown some
kind of explosive onto the bed. He reacted instinctively,
flinging himself to the floor as far from the bed as possible,
and burying his face in his hands.

Seconds passed, and there was no explosion. He raised his
head an inch to listen. From the direction of the bed came a
faint slithering sound. Don swore under his breath, rose to
his feet, and took a match out of his pants pocket. He bent
down to scrape it across the floor, and it burst into flame.
Its yellow light revealed what he had half-expected—the
sinuous coils of a snake. A rattler, plainly enough, but one
which had been shorn of its rattles.

Not many people can look at a snake without a feeling of
revulsion, and Don, despite the hundreds he had killed in his
life, was no exception. The hammer of his pistol was thumbed
back, and the gun pointed, before he stopped to think. Then
it occurred to him that there might be a better way of hand-
ling this. Someone had gone to a lot of trouble to make *him*
sweat; let *them* worry a little. He laid down the sixgun,
struck a fresh match, and swung the bed around next to the
window, being careful not to get within striking distance of
the snake, which had coiled and was eyeing him malevo-
lently.

Afterwards, he backed across the room, and, as he anticipated, the snake wriggled across the windowsill and dropped
to the roof below. It was the only rattler he had ever deliberately turned loose, but he was satisfied that it was as eager
to get away from civilization as he was to have it go.

The sky was beginning to turn gray in the east. Don didn't
like the idea of occupying a bed recently vacated by a snake
so he put on the rest of his clothes, buckled his gunbelt
around his waist, and moved the chair over beside the window. After a while he began to grin. Someone, so far he
didn't know who, had undoubtedly been paid for killing

him. When it turned out that he was still in good health, the situation could become embarrassing. And that could give him a clue as to who might be mixed up in this deal.

CHAPTER FOUR

SOME FOLKS, LIKE fine wine, mellow with age. Others, like vinegar, turn sour. Cletus Culver belonged to the latter group. Twenty years before, when he had come west from Indiana with his young bride, he had been an easygoing, rather diffident young man. Even then he had been ambitious, dreaming big dreams of owning a great cattle ranch someday, but his ambition had been leavened with humility.

It had taken him five years to discover that humility was not considered a virtue in this rough, lawless country. There was always somebody waiting to take advantage of anyone who showed signs of weakness. And the definition of weakness, in this raw land, had been broadened to include such qualities as honesty, fairness, and respect for the rights of others. A man tried to treat the Indians as equals and they robbed him blind; he allowed nesters to squat on his land and his small herd of cattle became even smaller.

What really triggered the change in Culver's philosophy was the untimely death of his wife in the summer of sixty-one. Never a robust woman, she had been in delicate health since the birth of their first child, Claire, during their first year in Arizona Territory. When the second girl was born, over three years later, it had been too much for her. She had died as she had lived, without uttering a complaint. But Culver felt that she could have survived had she received proper attention, if, for instance, she could have gone back to Indiana to have the baby, a trip which was impossible due to their meager finances.

It was too late to change things so far as his wife was concerned, but as the last clod fell on her cheap pine coffin, Culver swore to himself that neither of the daughters she had borne him would ever lack for anything that money could buy.

From that day forward, folks noticed a drastic change in the man. He had formerly been mild; now he was belligerent. Instead of turning the other cheek, he was liable to take offense when none was intended. The pistol, which he had frequently forgotten to wear, now became as much a part of his equipment as were his boots. Not only that, he spent long hours practicing with it, and would have spent more, except that he couldn't afford the cartridges. He lacked the natural ability to become a real gunslinger, but he became proficient enough so that men stepped out of his path rather than risk provoking him. The Reservation Indians learned to avoid his ranch as though it were contaminated with smallpox.

As Culver's personality changed, so did his finances. No one ever accused him of being dishonest, not even behind his back, but he took advantage of every opportunity to increase his worldly wealth. As he accumulated cash, he began lending it to less prosperous ranchers. His interest rates were as high as he could make them, and if one of his borrowers was unable to pay up on a due date, Culver foreclosed without a qualm. In his insatiable lust for money and the power which goes with it, he even built his own town, Paradise. Almost every one of its business establishments belonged to him, either fully or in part.

Now, seventeen years after his wife's death, nobody could deny that he had accomplished his avowed purpose. True, there were none who liked him any more, unless it was his foreman, and even that was questionable, but at least there was little likelihood that either of the girls would ever want for anything which money could buy. Certainly they never had, not since he had become successful. Claire, now twenty, had been back east attending school the last two years, and Minnie . . .

Culver hadn't opened his mouth since he and Whitey Larson had ridden out of town. Now he let out a curse which caused Larson to spur alongside and ask sharply, "Something wrong, Mr. Culver?"

"You know damn well what's wrong," Culver growled. "First that baby-faced bastard laying hands on Minnie, and now his goddam brother practically telling me to go to hell."

Larson didn't answer; experience had taught him that Culver didn't like to be interrupted. It was knowing things like this which made it possible for Larson to stay on as foreman of Culver's big outfit, after a dozen other men had given up in despair, or been kicked off the place. Larson knew when to keep still. He also remembered to say, "Mr. Culver," with the proper degree of respect. And, of course, he knew his job, which accounted for the good pay he was receiving. No one but Larson himself was aware that it wasn't the high pay which made him *want* to stay.

They had been riding through Culver's property for the last five miles, occasionally passing bunches of well-fed cattle wearing Culver's Box C brand. Now they came within sight of the ranch buildings themselves; a sprawling Spanish-type house and numerous smaller buildings. Three cowboys were washing up at the bench alongside the bunkhouse, getting ready for supper. A fourth was seated in the bunkhouse doorway, repairing a broken bridle. All of them turned to look, but nobody called a greeting. There was little friendliness between Culver and his hired hands. Except for emergencies, he hardly ever spoke to any of them, leaving it to Larson to relay his orders.

Culver dismounted in front of the house, tossed Larson his reins, and stomped across the veranda. He opened the thick wooden door and entered the front hall.

It was a house any man could be proud of, the rooms large and comfortable, with high beamed ceilings and panelled walls. Ordinarily, Culver derived considerable satisfaction out of it, but recently it had given him no pleasure. His mood wasn't helped any at the sight of his younger daughter walking hurriedly toward the part of the house in which her bedroom was situated. He called her name, and she turned quickly, feigning surprise.

"Yes, Papa? I didn't hear you come in."

She was a pretty girl, under normal circumstances, but she

had cried a good deal lately, which hadn't helped her looks. Also, her figure was misshapen, and would continue to get worse, according to Doc White, for another five months.

Now that he had called her, Culver didn't have anything to say. He had never been able to talk comfortably with Minnie, perhaps because her personality was so different from his own. She was inclined to be delicate, like her mother, and would rather stay in her room and read poetry than do the sort of things he considered important.

"Did you want to say something, Papa?"

"Just wondered how you were," he said stiffly. "Go ahead and do whatever you were going to. I'll see you at supper."

She turned away with relief, and presently passed out of sight into a hallway which opened off the far end of the room in which she had been sitting. Her father scowled in her direction several seconds after she was gone. One of the worst features of this whole dirty business was that he wasn't quite sure what had actually happened. Of course the Harding kid had deserved what he got, but had the idea been entirely his, as Minnie said? or had Minnie . . .

He shook his head angrily, threw his hat on a chair, and stepped from the front hall into the room Minnie had just left. It was what he always called the "setting" room, a carry-over from his Indiana upbringing. Whatever its correct name, it was four times as large as its Indiana counterpart. There were half a dozen spacious chairs, a huge square table on whose center rested an ornate coal oil lamp, a bookcase filled with the sort of trash that Minnie liked to read and that Culver wouldn't touch with a ten foot pole, and a high-backed leather sofa facing a big rock fireplace. All except the fireplace had been brought from Kansas City at great expense. About the only native articles in the room were the bright-colored Indian rugs.

As Culver reached the middle of the room, his older daughter, Claire, got up from the sofa, stretched like a languid cat, and said amusedly, "Don't tell me Minnie's got you buffaloed, Pa."

"What're you driving at?"

She shrugged.

"Never mind. Just something that struck me funny. What

happened in town? You rode out of here like you had a bee in your britches."

"Damn it, Claire, watch your language. You sound like one of Ruby Salmon's girls. What do they teach you, back east in that . . .?"

"So you know how Ruby's fallen angels talk," she said, grinning. "And all this time I've been under the impression you didn't realize what went on in that place."

Culver made a despairing gesture and dropped down on one of the chairs. He didn't see how two sisters could be so completely unlike—Minnie quiet and submissive and half the time living in a dream world of her own—Claire so confounded self-sufficient. It was too damned bad she hadn't been a boy. With a son like her, he could control the whole Territory.

Claire would have had her own viewpoint on that proposition. Being a man might have its advantages, she supposed, but being a woman was a lot more exciting—especially being a good-looking one. She had no false modesty about her own physical attributes. If she *had*, all she had to do was walk along the street, either here or in Philadelphia, and note the effect she had on any man who saw her.

She was also intelligent, and as determined as her father to get what she wanted. In fact, they had a number of characteristics in common, which might account for the frequency with which they clashed. However, instead of baiting him now, she said placatingly, "I didn't mean anything, Pa. It's just that this place could stand a little nonsense these days. Now tell me what took you to town in such a hurry."

There were very few people Culver could talk to nowadays—Whitey Larson, on certain subjects, and Claire, when she was in a reasonable mood. She seemed to be that way now, and since he wanted to blow off steam, he said savagely, "That damned Harding kid's brother rode into town today. Huddleson sent a man to tell me. Before I got there, he'd made the sheriff look like a fool, bullied Huddleson into letting him have a room at the hotel, and scared everybody else off the street."

Claire's eyes lighted with interest.

"What do you mean, he made the sheriff look like a fool?"

"Oh, Yankton said something he didn't like about his brother, and he called him a liar. Yankton went for his gun, but before he could get it in the open, this feller drew his own and like to broke the sheriff's wrist."

The girl grinned appreciatively.

"Sounds like quite a man, this Harding. Did you talk to him? What's he like?"

"Tough as hell," Culver said. "His looks? Well, I'd put him at about thirty. Maybe six feet tall, dark man ... say, what difference does it make what he looks like? He ain't going to be around long enough to be worth worrying about."

"Did you tell him so?"

Culver nodded morosely.

"I told him, and the damned fool asked if I was going to have him lynched like I did his brother."

"Did you?" Claire asked bluntly. "Have his brother lynched, I mean?"

"You know better than that, girl. I was right here in the house when it happened."

"But you didn't strain yourself trying to stop it, did you?"

"Why should I? That mob just saved me the trouble of going after him myself."

"From what you say about Sammy's brother, you might still be in for a little trouble." She frowned. "You say he's staying at the hotel?"

"He thinks he is, but I told Huddleson to figure some way to get him out." Culver looked up sharply. "If you've got some fool notion of looking this man over, you can forget it. I'm not letting any daughter of mine . . ."

"Oh, Lord, don't start that again. It isn't Minnie you're talking to. If I wanted to, I'd ride into town tonight, and the only way you could stop me would be by locking me in the icehouse. However, you don't need to worry. If he's half the man he sounds like, he'll do the looking. Once he finds out about me, that is."

Culver took a deep breath, and let it out slowly.

"You're too cocky for your own good," he said thickly. "One of these days you're going to make a mistake, and when you do . . ."

"When I do, it won't turn out the way it has with Minnie. If she'd only listened to me, she wouldn't be in this mess. I've tried for years to get her to carry a pistol when she's out by herself, but she wouldn't even let me teach her to shoot. Then she rides off alone without telling anybody where she's going, and the next thing we know, she's carrying a baby under her belt. If she felt like riding, why didn't she ask me to go along? Heaven knows I've asked *her* plenty of times." Claire shook her head disgustedly. "The way she acts, you'd almost think she *wanted* it to happen."

"Now what kind of a remark was that?"

"Skip it. I'm just relieving the pressure." She grinned. "What we need around here is a little excitement. I think I'll invite this one man army to pay us a visit. After all, he's practically a brother-in-law."

Without waiting for the explosion she was sure would follow, she left the room, going the same way Minnie had. What she had said about her sister hadn't been entirely in jest. It did seem almost impossible for any girl in her right mind to be taken advantage of so easily. Not only that, but Claire had seen Sammy Harding a few times, and he looked like the kind of boy Minnie would fall for—a polite, sensitive sort. Maybe he had even liked poetry. Was it possible that he and Minnie...? But in that case, why had Minnie made up this story about being dragged from her horse? And why had Sammy kept still about it?

Another possibility crossed her mind. Maybe Sammy Harding *hadn't* kept still. Only the men who had lynched him would know the truth about what he had said. If he had accused Minnie of being a willing partner, nobody would have dared repeat it for fear of Cletus Culver. Of course, if Minnie could be persuaded to talk ...

Minnie's door was closed, but Claire opened it and went in. She found her sister sitting in front of the dresser, listlessly examining her reflection in the mirror. She turned her head slowly and attempted a smile.

"I look terrible, don't I? According to Doc White . . ."

"Don't worry about it," Claire said, not unkindly. "You aren't the first girl that's ever had a baby. Once it's over,

you'll be as pretty as ever. Prettier, maybe. They say a
woman is never as beautiful as when she . . ."

"I wish you wouldn't talk about it," Minnie said dully.
"What difference does it make whether I'm pretty, or as
ugly as sin? I'll never look at a man again, and I hope nobody looks at me."

"You'll feel differently six months from now," Claire
promised. She actually felt sorry for her sister, though
she had long since despaired of ever understanding her.
"By the way, there's another Harding in town, an older
brother."

"An older brother?" Minnie said slowly, her cheeks pal-
ing. "You say he's in town—in Paradise?"

"Pa just talked to him," Claire told her. "Or maybe I
ought to say he talked to Pa. The way it sounds, he's a
pretty rugged individual. He outdrew Sheriff Yankton and
then didn't bother to shoot him. It seems the whole town's
staying off the streets, probably because most of them were
in that mob. They don't . . ."

Minnie didn't seem to be paying attention. She said again,
"You say he's in town? Do you think there's any danger
he'll come out here?"

"Not much chance of that, knowing what Pa would do
to him—with the help of the crew, of course. No, I don't
think he's especially interested in any of us Culvers. Probably he's here to take over the ranch his brother was
running."

"Oh dear God! I hope not," Minnie said tragically. "If
he stayed around, I don't think I could stand it. Every time
I had to go to town . . ."

"Don't lose any sleep over it. I imagine they'll figure
some way to get rid of him. If nothing else, maybe Pa can
buy him out. Pa's always wanting more land."

"I know," Minnie said, looking somewhat less forlorn.
"Speaking of that ranch, I wonder what's happened to it
in the last three months. If someone hasn't been looking
after things, it must be a mess."

"I believe someone said Sammy Harding had a man help-
ing him out. Probably he took over after Sammy—after
Sammy was gone. They call him Red something-or-other.
Martin, or Marlin; I don't know exactly."

Minnie was looking at her reflection again, and seemed to have lost interest in the subject, so Claire prepared to leave. At the doorway, she changed her mind and came back to lay a hand on Minnie's shoulder.

"We've never been very chummy, I'm afraid. But if there's anything I can do ... You know, you might want to talk to someone. And there's just Pa and me." She smiled at Minnie in the mirror. "What I'm trying to say is, if you have any sisterly confidence or anything, I'll be glad to lend an ear."

"Thank you," Minnie said. "I don't know what it'd be, but if there should be something, I'll remember."

"Good." This time, Claire actually left. This was about the closest they had ever come to acting like sisters, and she was a little reluctant to break it off. Even so, she couldn't help wondering. If Minnie had been having a love affair with Sammy Harding, and it had gotten out of hand ...

She made a disgusted gesture, and dismissed it from her mind, switching her thoughts to Sammy's older brother. Now *there* was a man she would like to meet. Too bad she hadn't thought to find out his first name.

CHAPTER FIVE

WHEN IT WAS light enough, Don poked his head out the window for a look at the roof below. As he had expected, the rattler had found a way of reaching the ground. By now, it was probably out on the desert, coiled beneath a clump of soapweed. He didn't envy the first person to come within striking distance of it. Rattlesnakes were not noted for their friendly dispositions, and this one would have more than average reason to hate humanity.

Daybreak came quickly, since there was nothing but flat prairie to the east. When the rim of the rising sun was far enough above the horizon for its rays to touch the ruffled pantaloons fluttering bravely from their makeshift flagpole, Don tossed his few belongings into the warbag, clamped it under his arm, and left the room, purposely leaving the door ajar. He descended the steps with as little noise as possible, crossed the unoccupied lobby, and went out onto the street.

This was the best time of the day; the air was still pleasantly cool and not yet contaminated with the dust which would later be raised by wagons and saddlehorses. Unfortunately, no one but Don seemed to be awake to enjoy it. He surveyed the street from the front of the hotel, then he moved out into the road and headed for the livery stable, his steps muffled by the soft dust. Someone in this town was due to be surprised, and he wanted it to be as much of a shock as possible.

Will Tully was apparently still in bed, but he had finished the job Don had given him. Sammy's headboard was leaning against the wall outside Tully's living quarters. Don studied it soberly for a moment, thinking how different things were from what he had anticipated. Just about now, he and Sammy should have been sitting down to breakfast together, making plans for today and for many more days to come. Instead, Sammy lay buried in an unmarked grave, lynched by the same men who had passed judgment on him.

Don swung his gaze to the other board, which Tully had nailed to the wall, and a tight smile twisted his lips. Perhaps this warning wouldn't insure the sanctity of Sammy's grave, but it would make somebody lose sleep. Before this was over, a lot of people were going to learn what it was to lie awake nights. Either that or they'd have to kill another Harding, which was something Don intended to make as difficult as possible.

He laid his warbag beside the boards, and crossed over to the stall in which his horse was stabled. The sorrel nuzzled his shoulder, and he talked to it softly for a moment before going to the rack for saddle and bridle. Minutes later he backed the animal out of its stall, paused long enough to pick up warbag and grave marker, and rode out.

It was an hour later when he returned from the graveyard and dismounted in front of the sheriff's office, and by
then the town had begun to come to life. A short, fat man
was sweeping the sidewalk in front of the general store, keeping his eyes on the walk as though he expected it to get
away from him. A buggy wheeled into town from the east,
and went into the livery stable. Seconds later, Doc White
trudged out of the barn, walking as though he were about
dead for sleep. Probably a newly-arrived-Arizonian was
squalling its protests in some nester's shack.

Before the doctor reached the hotel, a noise at Don's
back made him turn his head, and he saw Sheriff Yankton
regarding him sourly from the doorway of his office. There
was nothing about his attitude or expression which could
be interpreted as surprise, so apparently he knew nothing
about the rattlesnake.

The sheriff stepped out onto the sidewalk and said coldly,
"I see you're still in town, Harding. I'm beginning to think
you ain't very smart, or you would've pulled out during the
night."

"And lose all that good sleep?" Don countered. "Not
likely, Sheriff. Besides, you never did finish answering my
question yesterday. I'll ask it again. How do I get to
H Bar H?"

After a moment's hesitation, the sheriff jabbed a thumb
toward the east.

"Take the main road out of town. Half a mile out, there's
a pair of ruts turning north. The place you're looking for
is out about five miles."

"Much obliged," Don said. "I don't suppose you'd care
to join me for breakfast?"

"Not me, Harding. I'm particular who I eat with."

Don grinned.

"I'm not, Sheriff. That's how come I asked." He turned
away and entered the cafe next door.

There were two patrons at one of the tables, Will Tully
and a man who looked like a traveling salesman. Tully
nodded, and said, "I see you picked up your sign, Mr.
Harding. Was it all right?"

"Fine," Don told him. "By the way, I owe you for board-
ing my horse. How much?"

"Forget it, mister. You've paid me too much already."

Don grinned, but nevertheless reached in his pocket for a silver dollar. He laid it at Tully's place.

"Don't get the idea that I don't appreciate the offer, but word might get around that you'd done me a favor, and you'd probably end up getting a ride on a fencepost. Thanks just the same."

The drummer was staring at Don owlishly, and with something akin to fear, but he didn't say anything, so Don crossed to the table he had used the night before, and sat down in the same chair. After a moment, Helen Sprecher came out of the back room carrying Tully's and the drummer's breakfasts. She nodded at Don, got the other two men started, and came over to his table.

"Good morning, Mr. Harding."

"Morning, miss. Can a hungry man get some breakfast without too much trouble?"

"That's what I'm here for," she said, her tone courteous, but strictly impersonal. "You can have either bacon or beefsteak, with potatoes and eggs. And of course bread and coffee."

"No flapjacks?" Don asked. "I'd sure like to have . . ."

"Or flapjacks," she amended.

"Fair enough. Just bring me the whole works, while you're at it. I'm known as a pretty hearty eater."

"Very well." She seemed to be having difficulty maintaining her unsmiling demeanor as she turned toward the kitchen. Don had an idea she was a girl who preferred being friendly.

Tully and the salesman were busy with their food, paying no attention to anything else. Don looked past them at the front of the hotel. As he did, the hotel door opened, and Seth Huddleson came out onto the street, looking as though he hadn't had much sleep. He darted nervous glances up and down the road, then moved out from under the canopy and headed across toward the cafe.

Don watched him closely as he crossed the wooden sidewalk and opened the cafe door. Then Huddleson stepped into the room, saw Don seated at the table, and came to an abrupt stop. His eyes bulged, and his face turned livid. For a second it seemed that he would bolt, but before he could

make up his mind, Don crossed the room and grabbed his
arm.

"You're just in time to have breakfast with me, my
friend. I always like having company when I eat."

Huddleson tried to say something, but it came out as a
dry rattle. Before he could organize himself to resist, Don
had plunked him down at the table.

The hotelman seemed on the verge of panic. He continued
to stare at Don as though he couldn't believe his eyes.
Finally, however, he managed to get control of himself
enough to say weakly, "I'm not hungry, Mr. Harding. I was
just . . ." He faltered, then went on quickly. "I was just
looking for somebody."

His guilt was obvious enough to be almost comical, but
Don chose to ignore it. If Huddleson had arranged for the
snake to be thrown into his room, he had only been a tool
of someone else. Just as the man who had actually tossed
the snake had been a tool of Huddleson. Don couldn't con-
ceive of Huddleson having the courage to handle the snake
himself. In the back of Don's mind was the recollection of
that brief talk Cletus Culver had had with the hotelman
before leaving town. But there was no use questioning the
man about it now. He would only deny it; as frightened as
he was of Don at the moment, he was probably even more
afraid of Culver.

"At least have a cup of coffee," Don urged. "Whoever
you're looking for won't leave town in the next fifteen
minutes. Besides, I'm glad you came in. It'll save me
crossing the street to tell you I won't be using that room
tonight. I'll be staying out at the ranch from now on."

Huddleson's hand trembled as he wiped it across his
mouth. He moistened his lips, and said thickly, "The room
was all right, wasn't it? I mean you didn't . . ."

"I slept like a log," Don lied. "Oh, I did wake up once
in the night. Thought I heard something under the bed,
but it was probably a mouse. By the way, I left the door
open so you'd know I was gone, in case you wanted somebody to go in and straighten up."

Huddleson's hands gripped the edge of the table, and he
pushed back his chair.

"I'm sorry, Mr. Harding, but I just can't even drink a

cup of coffee. Fact is, I ain't feeling so good this morning."
He stood up.

This time, Don didn't stop him. Just for a second, he almost pitied the man, in spite of what had happened in the night. As long as Huddleson believed there was a rattlesnake loose in the hotel, he wouldn't make a move without being afraid of stepping on it. But Huddleson's terror could start a chain reaction which would eventually reach the one at the top. And when it did, someone might get careless and make a mistake.

Don watched Huddleson scurry across the street and open the hotel door. Before going any farther, the little man stuck his head through the opening and peered around. Only then did he go inside.

Grinning, Don looked around and saw Helen Sprecher watching him from the kitchen doorway. She brought his breakfast to the table, and asked accusingly, "What did you say to Mr. Huddleson? He went out of here like a scared rabbit."

Don shrugged, and said innocently, "Me? I didn't say anything. All I did was invite him to have breakfast with me. I thought maybe that was the way he always acted."

"All right, if you don't want to tell me." She set down his coffee so hard that some of it sloshed out of the cup. "I've got a feeling, Mr. Harding, that this town will breathe a lot easier after you leave."

"Then it won't have long to wait," Don said. "Because I intend to ride out just as soon as I finish this breakfast."

The sheriff had told the truth about at least one thing. Half a mile out of town there was a road angling to the right. A pair of ruts, really, as Yankton had said. Don swung the sorrel onto it, and twisted sideways in the saddle for a last look at the town. Even from this slight distance, Paradise seemed small. As small, he told himself bleakly, as the folks who lived there. He focused his eyes on the graveyard, and imagined that he could pick out Sammy's freshly erected marker.

Perhaps two miles from where it had branched off, the road climbed to the top of a low ridge. Beyond and below lay a small valley—small as sizes were reckoned in this part of the country. Running down the center of it was a strip of green which presumably marked the path of the river Sammy had written about.

Don reined up to look at it, and incidentally to rest his mount. With his eyes he followed the course of the stream from its source in the foothills down through the valley to a point at which it disappeared around a curve in the hill he was on. If he remembered the descriptions in the deed, H Bar H land extended from the foothills on the north to the main east-west road on the south, and from one rim of the valley to the other. A small spread, compared to some on which he had worked, but plenty big for two men to operate. One man now, he corrected himself; no doubt he would have to hire help if he hoped to make a go of it.

From the ridge on which he had paused, the road wound down into the valley, sand giving way to waves of yellow grass in the bottomland which presumably had the benefit of more water during the rainy season, and where the snow would lay longer on the ground in the spring. In spite of the unfortunate circumstances under which he was arriving, Don couldn't help getting a little excited at what he saw. It was country to delight the heart of any real cattleman, and most of his life he had been associated with the cattle business in some capacity.

One thing bothered him. So far, he had seen no sign of a dwelling. According to Sammy's letters, there was a small cabin on the place, adequate for their needs until they had time to build a real house.

He had his answer when he rode through a little bunch of trees into a clearing where there was a pile of ashes and a jumble of charred logs. From the fact that no weeds had as yet gained a foothold, he knew the fire had taken place not long before. This was evidently the cabin Sammy had written about, probably burned by the men who had lynched him.

His brief moment of pleasure over, Don dismounted and moved up for a closer look at the ruins. As he did, a voice said tightly, "Don't reach for your gun, mister. You're lined up in my sights."

Don stayed as he was while someone moved up behind him and lifted the pistol out of his holster. It was a fool thing to have done, he told himself angrily, allowing someone to get close enough to get the drop on him.

"You can turn around now if you want to, but don't try anything."

Don turned slowly, and saw a young man squinting at him along the barrel of a rifle; he was hardly more than a boy. His most outstanding characteristic was a mop of unruly red hair. Other than that, he looked like anybody else in this part of the country; scuffed boots, faded denims, a gray cotton shirt, and a shapeless hat which had once been black.

"What's your name, mister, and what're you doing in this valley?"

There seemed to be more likelihood of the boy's pulling the trigger out of nervousness than out of deliberate intent, so Don was careful to keep his voice low when he said, "My name's Harding, and I just..."

"Harding!"

The boy reacted so violently to the name that Don was afraid he'd pull the trigger without meaning to. Then the boy relaxed a little, and said more calmly, "What's your first name, mister?"

"Don. I'm Sammy Harding's brother."

The boy hesitated a few seconds, then lowered the barrel of the rifle.

"If your name's really Harding, maybe you've got some way of proving it."

"Sure I have," Don told him. "Sammy's last letter is in my shirt pocket, if that'll satisfy you. Or you can ask me anything about him you want to know, and I'll try to answer."

"Well—you might start by telling me what he looked like."

"All right. He had light brown hair, blue eyes, and weighed around one fifty. As to his age, he'd be twenty years old—about the same age you are, I imagine."

"I'm nineteen," the boy volunteered. "Anything else?"

"Good Lord, boy! How much do you need? Even if I weren't Sammy's brother, what is there to get excited about? Are you afraid I'm going to dig through these ashes and find a silver spoon or something?"

"No, I suppose you ain't," the boy admitted. "I reckon you're Sammy's brother, too. He talked about you a lot, said you were big and tough, and looked about the way you do." He shifted the gun to his left hand, and held out his right. "I'm Luke Marlowe, Mr. Harding. Everybody calls me Red."

"I wonder why," Don said, smiling, and took Red's hand. "Sorry I surprised you, but I wasn't expecting to find anybody. Now you tell me something. How come you're so well acquainted with my brother?"

"I was working for him," Red Marlowe said. "He hired me about a month before . . ." His young face drew into grim lines. "Those dirty bastards! If they'd come an hour later, me and Sammy would've both been here. Then maybe . . ."

"No use worrying about it now," Don said. "I suppose you know what they claim he did."

"Sure, but it's a stinkin' lie. Sammy wouldn't've done a thing like that for a million dollars. Why he hated to slap a brand on a calf, for fear of hurting it. He would no more mistreat a girl than he'd rob a bank or something."

"I'm glad to find someone who agrees with me," Don said. He bent down to pick up his gun where Red had dropped it, blew dust out of the cylinder, and slid it back into his holster. "Tell me, Marlowe, with Sammy dead, how does it happen you're still here?"

"Sammy told me you'd be coming, Mr. Harding. I figured to keep an eye on things till you showed up. You know, make sure no cows got stuck in a hole or anything."

"Sure," Don said. He looked at the boy with new interest. Red Marlowe's appearance wasn't impressive, but anyone who would take it upon himself to watch out for another man's property must have a good deal of character. To test it, Don took out his moneypouch and said, "You can't afford to work for nothing, Marlowe. How much do I owe you?"

"Aw hell," Marlowe said embarrassedly. "You don't owe me nothing. Me and Sammy got to be pretty good friends. Besides, I didn't have anything else to do. Not until fall roundup, anyway, when the big outfits start hiring."

"Then how about working for me? Until something better comes along, that is."

"For you?" The boy's face lighted in a grin. "Sure, Mr. Harding, if you really mean it. There's nothing I'd like better."

"Then it's a deal. Only from now on, you're going to be

paid. And another thing, let's forget this 'Mr. Harding' stuff. My friends call me Don."

"And I'm just 'Red', Mr.—I mean Don."

"Good." Don knew that Red Marlowe would be a poor substitute for Sammy, but it would be good to have someone to talk to. And Red had known Sammy, which meant he wasn't exactly a stranger.

"There's just one thing, Red. I've already been ordered to leave the country. This job of yours may not last long enough for you to get tired of it."

Red frowned, and said knowingly, "Did Cletus Culver tell you, maybe?"

"That's right. Do you know the man?"

"Only by sight. Some of our H Bar H cows drifted onto Culver's land once, and when I was bringing them back, Culver and that ramrod of his happened along. Culver accused me of being a cow-thief. I believe he would've taken a shot at me if his foreman hadn't talked him out of it. Larson—that's the foreman's name—took a closer look at the cows and told him they'd never worn a Box C brand." Red shook his head wryly. "I wouldn't say me and Culver was very good friends. No sir."

"Then that makes two of us," Don said, and slapped the boy's thin shoulder. "We won't worry about Culver until we have to. Right now, let's talk about this ranch."

"Yes, sir," Red said. "But maybe it'd be better if I just showed it to you. I ain't so good at talking. I've got a horse over beyond that brush heap. If you'll wait here a minute, I'll go get him."

CHAPTER SIX

RED'S MOUNT PROVED to be a wild-eyed pinto. It was a little flashy for Don's personal taste, but he supposed the boy had never been in a situation where he didn't want to present a good target for some ambusher. Also, Don could remember back to the time when he had been nineteen himself, and had been more interested in show than in more practical considerations. Anyway, he didn't make it a practice to volunteer advice, so he offered none now. It did occur to him, however, to ask if there were any other horses in the H Bar H corral.

"There ain't even a corral," Red said wryly. "All we had was two horses, this one and Sammy's. We kept 'em in a lean-to shed hooked to the cabin. It went up in smoke with the rest of it."

"And Sammy's horse?"

"They must've used it to haul him to town. Anyway, I ain't seen anything of it since." Red looked around uneasily. "Maybe I shouldn't've put it that way, Don. What I meant ..."

"It's all right. Keeping still about what happened won't change things. I take it they lynched him here on H Bar H?"

"Yes, sir." Red pointed to a little grove of pines about a mile to the north. "Right up there is where they done it. The same bunch of trees where we got the logs for the lean-to."

Don followed the direction of Red's pointing finger, and was pretty sure he could pick out the tree they had used, one which was taller than the others, and had a thick branch about ten feet from the ground. He stared at it a few seconds, then said quietly, "This horse of Sammy's—what did it look like?"

"It was a bay with white stockings on all four feet. There's a better way of spotting him, though. Sammy got me to throw his brand on its left front shoulder."

"We'll get it back," Don promised. "Now let's see the rest of the spread."

Three hours later, after riding up one side of the stream to the foothills, and back on the other, Don was more impressed than before with the ranch's potentialities. However, he was also more sharply aware of the obstacles to be surmounted before it could be turned ino a paying proposition. The land itself was all he could have asked for, and the water supply, to judge from the depth of the stream now, should be ample. Except for these two features, however, there was nothing—no buildings, no horses, and no tools. Furthermore, during the course of the ride, they had seen only a dozen H Bar H cattle. He questioned Red about this.

"There ain't many," Red admitted. "When Sammy hired me, he was supposed to have almost a hundred head, stuff that was on the ranch when you and him bought it. I never saw that many myself, but there used to be a lot more than we saw today. Ever since Sammy's been gone, they seem to be disappearing." He frowned. "Of course, some of 'em may have drifted over the ridge to Culver's property. After what happened to me that once, I wasn't so crazy about going after 'em alone."

"Nobody could blame you for that," Don assured him. "Does Culver's property adjoin H Bar H all along our west side?"

"Yes, sir. Of course, his land keeps on a lot farther south than yours. Hell, he must have a hundred square miles."

"And I suppose our missing cows might be anyplace on it," Don said. "Well, that's something else we can worry about later. That, and getting Sammy's horse back. Right now we wouldn't have time to fool with any more cattle anyway. Not until we build us some kind of a house, and lay in a few supplies. I don't suppose there's such a thing as an ax on the place?"

"There was," Red said. "Maybe there still is, if we dig through the ashes."

"Then let's start digging. I sure don't crave to cut those logs with my teeth." He swung the sorrel toward the site of the burned cabin.

When he entered the clearing, he pulled up sharply at the sight of a man sitting on the ground with his back against a rock.

The man didn't act at all surprised, nor did he seem to anticipate that anyone would question his right to be there. He had been whittling on a chunk of wood, and he continued to do so, interrupting his labors only long enough to glance up at the approaching riders.

Don waited for him to speak; when he didn't, he let

the sorrel carry him a few steps farther, where he stopped for a closer inspection.

It was hard to estimate the man's age. His face was the color of a well worn boot, but the long hair visible beneath his sweat-stained hat showed no trace of gray. As to his clothes, they were about the most disreputable Don had ever seen; faded and patched denim pants, brush-scarred boots, a nondescript flannel shirt, and a grease-stained deer-hide jacket. The man himself looked almost as bad. A half inch of stubble covered his jaw, and it appeared that it had been some time since he had associated with soap and water. The only exceptions to this were his hands, which were small and surprisingly clean.

The stranger added a few final touches to whatever it was he was carving, shoved the blade of the knife down inside his right boot, and rose to his feet. His changed position brought into view a holstered gun dangling against his right leg. He grinned up at Don and held out the piece of wood he had been working on.

"Not bad, hey? And just an hour ago it was nothing but a chunk of dead wood."

Don reached down to take it, and turned it over slowly in his fingers. It was approximately the size and shape of an egg, but with a knob on one end and a square depression cut into the other. He frowned, and shifted his eyes to the stranger, who appeared to be waiting for some kind of comment.

"It's a nice job of carving, all right, but what's it good for?"

"Not a damned thing," the stranger said happily. "It's just like me, pretty as hell but no damn good." He reached up for it, and tossed it toward the creek. "You know something, mister? A lot of folks would've made out they knew what it was for. It's funny how people hate to admit they're stumped. Could be you're not so dumb as the average."

"Thanks," Don said dryly.

"You're welcome." He pointed his chin past Don toward where Red Marlowe had pulled up at the edge of the clearing.

"You might as well put that rifle back in the scabbard, sonny. I ain't going to start no trouble. Not an old washed

out has-been like me. Even if I wanted to, this old bogleg
of mine would likely fall apart." He glanced down at the
holstered gun, which did indeed look as though there were
little to hold it together.

In spite of the man's bedraggled appearance, there was
something about him which Don liked. He grinned down
at him, and said good-naturedly, "All right, you've convinced us that you and your gun are no earthly use. Now
how about telling us who you are?"

"Well, since you ask." He bared his teeth in a grin.
"Meet the Kelso Kid, mister; that's me."

"And I'm Don Harding," Don said, reaching down to
take the man's hand. "My friend here is named Red Marlowe."

The Kelso Kid acknowledged the introduction with a nod,
and withdrew his hand from Don's grip. His handclasp had
been firm enough, but once again Don was struck with the
incongruity of those uncalloused palms. This man certainly
didn't earn his living by doing hard physical labor.

The Kid was eyeing Don narrowly.

"Harding, hey? Does that make you a relative of the boy
they murdered?"

"His brother," Don said, and added, "You just now used
the word 'murdered'. Does that mean you know Sammy
wasn't guilty of anything?"

"All I know . . ." the Kid said, then let it drop. "Hell,
mister, how would I know anything about it? The way I
look at it, lynching's the same as murder; it's killing a man
without giving him an even break. That's all I meant."

"You were about to say something else," Don told him.
"What was it?"

"Don't know what you're talking about," the Kid
grumbled. "Damn it, try to do a feller a favor, and he
jumps down your throat."

"You're right," Don admitted. "I spoke out of turn."
He frowned. "This favor you mentioned—what was it?"

"Favor?" The Kid scratched his jaw. "Oh yes, I remember. It's about that horse of your brother's. Was it a bay
with four white feet?"

"So I've been told."

"Figured it might be," the Kid said. "None of my business, but I don't hold with horse-stealing, even from a dead man." He grinned. "Don't get me wrong, it ain't that I'm so all-fired honest. You take busting into a bank, now, or holding up a stagecoach—but stealing a horse . . ." He shook his head.

"About Sammy's bay?" Don prompted.

"I'm getting to that. Strikes me I saw a horse like that in town. Seems as if it was in Sheriff Yankton's barn." He looked up quickly. "Now don't you tell anyone I said so. That sheriff, he's a tough customer. He's got me scared."

Don had an idea that nobody had the Kelso Kid very scared, but he merely said, "I'll leave your name out of it. Much obliged for the information."

"Sure, mister." He added solemnly, "Not that I'd want to make trouble for the sheriff . . ." His voice trailed off in a vast yawn and he reached inside his shirt to scratch. "Well, I'd better be going. Got a lot of important business to neglect." He nodded toward the burned cabin. "You fellers fixing to put up a new one?"

"That's right," Don acknowledged, and added as an afterthought, "You're welcome to help, if you're looking for a few days' work."

"Work!" The Kid looked shocked. "Hell, man, I've got my pride. Suppose it got around that the Kelso Kid was working for wages? What'd folks think?" He turned and walked away around a bend in the trail. Seconds later there was the sound of a running horse.

Don grinned, and turned to look at Red Marlowe.

"What do you make of our friend there? Have you ever seen him before?"

"No, sir, and if I never see him again, it'll be too soon. What was he up to, anyway? That's what I'd like to know. Like as not, somebody sent him to spy on us."

"In that case," Don commented, "he didn't find out much." He swung down from his saddle, and tied the reins to a bush. "Anyway, he told us about Sammy's horse. It looks as if I'll be seeing that sheriff again sooner than I'd expected. Now let's look for that ax."

"Yes, sir," Red said, and got down to join him, continuing to slant uneasy glances in the direction the Kelso Kid had taken.

They managed to locate the ax-head without too much trouble, and Don fashioned a new handle for it. After that, they got busy on preparations for the new cabin. Don rode to the grove of pines, leaving Red to clean away the debris and to salvage anything possible.

At the pines, Don looked up grimly at the lowest branch of the tallest tree. Rope marks were still visible, and his lips tightened in a hard line. He was tempted to chop down this reminder of his brother's death, but a stronger impulse prompted him to leave it as it was. When Sammy's name had been cleared, and his murder avenged, the tree could come down. He dismounted and went to work on one of the others. Anger added strength to his muscles, and the valley echoed with the sound of the ax.

By dusk, when he returned to the clearing, all that remained of the old cabin was the stone fireplace, which they could use in the new one. In the process of clearing away the debris, Red had uncovered a few things they could salvage, including the metal part of a shovel. There was also a rifle without any stock, but Don decided not to repair it; since the steel had probably lost its temper in the fire, it would be liable to explode if the gun were fired.

Don had a few provisions in his saddlebags, and Red produced a small supply of his own. They considered trying to augment their supper with some fish from the stream, but decided that they were more tired than hungry. As soon as they had finished eating, they rolled up in their blankets and went to sleep.

Don awoke just before sunup, and lay quietly for a few minutes, listening to the gurgle of the stream and the occasional splash of a fish leaping for a bug. Some distance away, a woodpecker started hammering away in search of its breakfast. Don turned to look, and his eyes fell on the tree from which Sammy had been hanged. Instantly the spell was broken, and he rolled to his feet.

Red Marlowe was curled up like a child, his knees doubled up against his chest. Don decided to let him sleep a few minutes longer while he moved the horses. He went as quietly as possible toward the meadow in which they were picketed.

There were no horses there. Don stiffened and let his hand

drop to his gun, then moved it away as he realized that whoever had been here had no doubt long since left. He moved ahead to the middle of the little swale, hoping against hope that he was mixed up as to the location.

There was no use kidding himself; this was the right spot. He spun on his heel and started back toward camp, then as a horse snuffled, he came to an abrupt stop. The sound apparently came from across the creek. At about the same time, Red Marlowe came into sight from the direction of the clearing.

Don motioned him to silence, and moved over beside him. Keeping his voice low, he explained what had happened. Since Red was unarmed, Don told him to go back to the clearing and get his rifle. Meanwhile, he would try to get across the stream without being spotted.

With drawn gun, he waded across, his eyes probing the underbrush along its bank. He made the other side safely, and parted the branches with his left hand.

What he saw made him first curse and then break out into a laugh. Red's horse, and his own were grazing peacefully at the ends of their picket ropes. It wasn't this which had made him laugh, but the appearance of the picket pins to which they were tied. Both wooden stakes were elaborately carved, their tops shaped like duncecaps. It was obviously the work of the Kelso Kid. While Don and Red had slept, the Kid had calmly made off with their horses.

The Kelso Kid seemed like a man who could enjoy a good joke, but Don was satisfied that he hadn't gone to all this trouble just for a laugh. For some reason, he had wanted to demonstrate how vulnerable they were. If *he* could get close enough to steal their horses, so could someone else. Instead of telling them so, and perhaps inviting an argument, he had used the direct method. Why he had bothered about it, Don couldn't guess.

From across the creek, Red yelled anxiously, "Are you all right, Don?"

"Sure, and I found our horses. I'll bring them back."

There was no reason to tell Red Marlowe what had happened. Red was already leery of the Kelso Kid, and this might make him worse. From now on, Don would make sure that they took greater precautions, but it wouldn't help any for Red's nerves to be on edge. You never knew how a boy his age might react.

Don pulled the picket pins, untied the ropes, and tossed the pins into the brush. He shortened up the ropes and led the two horses back across the creek, Red's pinto fighting him every step of the way.

"What happened?" Red wanted to know.

"I guess they felt like seeing what it was like on the other side," Don told him. "Maybe the ground where we drove those stakes wasn't as solid as it looked. Anyway, we're lucky they didn't go farther. Now let's tie 'em up and get some breakfast."

"Yes, sir," Red said, still looking puzzled. "It's the first time I ever knew that pinto to cross a creek when he didn't have to."

Don didn't comment, and by the time breakfast was over, the boy seemed to have forgotten it. Afterwards, there was little time to think about anything except work. Between them they managed to cut enough logs so that, together with the ones cut the day before, they would be able to build the small cabin Don had in mind. By dark, they had finished dragging them to the clearing.

This night they took turns standing guard, and, of course, nothing happened except that they were both sleepy the next morning. However, by suppertime they had succeeded in raising the sides of the cabin to a height of six feet. Now, all that remained was the addition of a roof, and construction of a shelter for the horses.

It wouldn't be much of a cabin, just a roughly square structure nine feet each way. By building one side of it around the fireplace, they had saved a week's work. There was a doorway opposite the fireplace, a little to one side of center, but as yet, no door. Instead of windows, Don had notched one log on each side of the cabin to form portholes. He had an idea that they might be glad to sacrifice a little light and ventilation for an increased margin of safety. The notches were the height of a man's shoulder, and would accommodate a rifle barrel.

Red had proved to be a good worker, and one who could follow instructions. If he didn't seem especially enthusiastic about the work they were doing, it was only natural. After all, it wasn't as though he were working for himself. Besides, it was entirely possible that he couldn't forget what had happened to Sammy. Apparently he still blamed himself for having been away when the mob rode into the clearing. No doubt he and Sammy had been good friends.

They ate supper in the cabin that night, with only the smoke from the fireplace to blot out the stars. Afterwards, Don outlined his plans for the following day. He had decided that it would be necessary to go to town for supplies. Both his and Red's larders were depleted, and there was no spare time for hunting and fishing. Even more important, they would need some spikes for the door, and nails for the roof.

"Anything special you want me to do while you're away?" Red asked.

"You might cut some beams for the roof," Don suggested. "Try to pick out straight ones if you can."

Red nodded, and inquired, "How long do you expect to be gone?"

"That depends. If I don't run into trouble, I ought to be back by noon. On the other hand, if I do . . ."

Red looked up sharply.

"Trouble? Just buying some supplies?"

"It sounds simple enough, doesn't it? In spite of what Cletus Culver said. But what I have in mind is something a little different. I aim to come back with Sammy's horse."

CHAPTER SEVEN

INSTEAD OF TAKING the most direct route to town, Don elected to ride along the western border of H Bar H. It would take only an hour or so longer, and would give him an opportunity to become familiar with a section of the ranch which he hadn't yet seen. He left the

cabin as soon as it was light enough to ride, splashed his
horse across the creek, and rode toward the ridge which
marked the line between his property and Cletus Culver's.
  From atop the rise, he turned to look back at the valley.
Smoke still spiraled upward from the fireplace chimney,
and Red Marlowe could be seen saddling the pinto preparatory to going after roof timbers. From this distance
he could have been any young cowhand; Don was irre-
sistably reminded that his brother, who should have been
there with Red, would never again fork a horse, or work,
or laugh, or enjoy a fire of an evening.
  Now that it was too late to do anything about it, he re-
gretted that he and Sammy had spent so little time together, though, to be perfectly fair, it hadn't been his fault.
After the folks had died, it had been up to him to earn
a living for both of them. This hadn't been much of a
problem, since at seventeen he was already as big as many
mature men, and was accustomed to hard work. But there
was no way for a cowboy to keep his brother with him in
a bunkhouse or on roundup, so it had been necessary to
leave Sammy in the care of friendly townfolk who had
been glad to earn the small payment Don had offered.
Dollars had been scarce in Kansas in those days.
  Of course, there had been another reason for letting
Sammy stay in town. Don himself had received very little
formal schooling, and for that reason was determined that
Sammy should do better. Especially since it was evident that
Sammy was cut out for better things than a lifetime of
punching cows. Even buying this ranch had been part of
Don's plan to provide the boy with an opportunity to
amount to something. A cowhand, even a foreman such
as Don had become, could hardly hope to earn enough
money to pay for a college education. If the ranch could
be made to succeed . . .
  Don put a curb on his thoughts. All that was water over
the dam, now. No use brooding over what might have
been. He turned his back on the scene below, and touched
spurs to the sorrel.
  The line between H Bar H and Box C was of course an
imaginary one, but as Don looked to the west, he knew
he was grazing at Culver property. The grass up on this

higher level was not as thick as that down in the valley, but since Culver owned so much of it, he undoubtedly had enough graze for an immense herd. In fact, a few scattered bunches of cows were visible even from here.

Farther off, from beyond a low hummock, a plume of smoke lifted against the sky. This would be from the cookstove in Culver's house, Don supposed—in the house where the girl lived who was responsible for Sammy's lynching.

For a moment, Don considered riding over there right now, and meeting her face to face. Then his better judgment asserted itself and he dismissed the idea. Culver had threatened to kill him if he came within a mile of his daughter. It would be worth the risk if there were a chance of accomplishing anything. But the odds were against his even seeing her, and even if he surmounted that obstacle, there was no reason to expect that she would talk to him. Or, if she did, that she would tell the truth.

He came within sight of the main east-west road which ran into town. As he did, a buggy appeared some distance to the west, leaving a stream of dust in its wake. It caught up to him as he reached the road, and he was surprised to see a woman holding the reins. He was even more surprised when she pulled the team alongside, and gave him a flashing smile.

"Mr. Harding?"

Don nodded, and kneed the sorrel closer to the buggy. He saw a strikingly handsome young woman who returned his look with frank curiosity. There was nothing in her attitude to indicate that she considered it unusual for a woman to start a conversation with a man she had never met.

"My name's Harding, all right," Don said, "but I'm afraid you've got the advantage of me. Am I supposed to know..."

"Don't apologize, Mr. Harding; we've never met." She seemed to be amused at some secret joke which was about to make her laugh. "Of course we really should know each other, I suppose, inasmuch as your brother and my sister..."

"Is your name Culver?"

She nodded, and would have said more, but Don touched his hatbrim, wheeled the sorrel, and rode off toward town.

He hadn't gone ten yards when the buggy caught up with him, and the girl called tauntingly, "What's the matter, Mr. Harding? Don't tell me a man who can get the best of Sheriff Yankton is afraid of a girl!"

Don rode straight on as though he hadn't heard her, keeping his eyes to the front.

"Why damn you!"

It struck Don that those were the exact words used by Cletus Culver that day in the cafe. Spoken in almost the same tone, too, that of a landowner talking to a slave. Even so, he would have ignored it, except that she cut the team in front of him, forcing him either to stop or to get off the road. He turned and saw her glaring at him angrily.

"Apparently you're short on manners, Mr. Harding. I was talking to you."

"Chances are I am, ma'am, but I try not to be short on common sense." He glanced back along the road, then met her angry eyes. "Just what does your father expect to accomplish by this little performance? Is it supposed to lead to another lynching party?"

"My father? Don't talk like a fool. Why would my father. . .?"

"He ordered me to leave town," Don said. "I seem to recall something about there being ways of making me leave, in case I didn't follow orders." His lips twisted in a wry grin. "It strikes me that you Culvers are accustomed to having things pretty much your own way, regardless of who gets hurt. Now, if you'll just get this rig out of my path. . ."

She made no move to comply, but said icily, "Do you actually think this was my father's idea?"

"Let's put it this way, ma'am. I sure don't think it was just coincidence, our meeting the way we did. You don't impress me as the kind of woman to go buggy-riding so early in the day, especially"—he pointed at the tight pants she was wearing—"especially wearing riding britches."

She glanced down at her legs, and lost some of her assurance.

"All right, Mr. Harding, so it wasn't a coincidence. I was out for my morning ride when I saw you on the ridge. There was time to go back for the buggy, and I did. Does that satisfy you?"

"Not quite. For one thing, how come you had to get the rig? Couldn't you have ridden out here...?"

"Damn it, I was going to invite you to tie your horse behind, and finish the ride in comfort, if you hadn't been so confounded suspicious." She hauled back on the lines, pulling the team out of Don's path. "Any more questions?"

"Just one," Don said, and pointed back the way she had come. "If all you say is true, how do you account for *that*?"

She leaned out the side of the buggy and looked back. Coming up fast was a solitary rider, his horse raising a great cloud of dust. As he drew nearer, he became recognizable as Whitey Larson, the Box C foreman.

Don eased his mount away from the buggy, so as to have greater freedom of action, and loosened the gun in his holster. He was vaguely aware of some exasperated comment from the girl, but his attention was concentrated on Larson. The Box C ramrod didn't look like the kind of man who would push his horse at this speed without good reason.

Larson brought his horse to a sliding stop alongside the back wheel of the buggy. There was anger in his eyes, and some other emotion which Don couldn't interpret. He flashed a quick look at Don, who was sitting easily in the saddle, waiting for Larson to make the first move.

"You can slack off, Harding; I'm not here looking for trouble."

"Glad to hear it," Don said, but he maintained his attitude of watchful waiting.

Larson apparently noticed this, for he smiled briefly before turning toward the girl, who was frowning at him from beneath the buggy top.

"Your pa wants you at the house, Miss Claire. He asked me to fetch you."

"Oh he did, did he? Well, you can go back and tell Pa I'll be home when I'm good and ready. Who does he think I am, an infant to order around like he would Minnie?"

"I'm sorry, Miss Claire, but he gave me my orders." Larson was obviously uncomfortable, but he showed no signs of backing down. "All he told me to do was bring you home."

Evidently the girl realized the futility of arguing, for she sighed resignedly, gathered up the lines, and started to turn the rig. Then, without any warning, she snatched the whip out of its socket and laid it across the team's rumps. The horses bolted toward town.

The sudden commotion made Don's sorrel jump. Larson's mount, responding even more violently, reared up on its hind legs, almost dismounting its rider. The Box C foreman fought his horse under control and took off after the buggy.

Don had been temporarily relegated to the role of spectator. He turned his horse toward town and followed at a more conservative speed, curious to see how this was going to end.

Despite the girl's headstart, Larson overtook her before she reached the edge of town. He drew even with her horses' heads, and leaned down to grab the near bridle, dragging the team to a stop.

"Damn you, Whitey!" Claire screamed. "Get your hands off that strap, or so help me. . ."

Don was close enough to see the set of Larson's jaw, and was satisfied that he intended to follow Culver's order regardless of the consequences. Then the buggy-whip flashed, and Larson's head jerked as the leather laid a welt across his cheek.

The whip whistled again, but this time, Larson succeeded in grabbing it. He gave it a sudden jerk, and Claire, who was apparently determined not to let go, was yanked out of the buggy and spilled on her face in the road. She scrambled to her feet and snatched a small nickle-plated pistol out of her pocket. Before she could cock it, Larson vaulted from his saddle and knocked the gun out of her hand.

"You crazy spoiled little fool! I've killed men for less than that. Now get your damned butt back on that seat and head for the ranch, or so help me I'll drag you home on the end of a rope!"

For a moment, Claire only stared at him in stunned astonishment. Then she turned to Don, who had pulled up not far away.

"You heard that," she said thinly. "Are you going to sit there and let him get away with it?"

"No, ma'am, I certainly am not. I'm riding on into town." He grinned down at her. "If you want a little free advice, which I'm pretty sure you don't, you'd be smart to get back in that buggy before your friend thinks of a good place to apply that whip." He touched his hat, nodded courteously to Whitey Larson, and rode into town wondering if he had correctly interpreted the way Larson was looking at Claire Culver. If he had, he was sorry for the man, especially if Claire was aware of how Larson felt.

The fat little merchant, who had been sweeping in front of the general store at the time of Don's last visit, was once again out on the sidewalk, leaning on his broom and peering at the commotion on the road. Before Don came within speaking distance, the man hurried back inside, leaving half the walk unswept.

Don pulled up in front of the store, and looked up at the faded sign, which read "General Merchandise, Niles Dowdall, Prop., Groceries, Hardware, Feed and Grain, Clothing and Misc."

This would presumably be the place to buy the things he needed at H Bar H. Don stepped down from the saddle, and looped his reins around the warped hitchrail.

Inside the store, he was met by the characteristic smells of leather and denim, vinegar and cheese, cinnamon and coal oil. A swarm of gnats hovered over an open pickle barrel. A huge yellow tomcat was crouched on top of a pile of sacked grain, watching Don through slitted eyes.

The place seemed to be well equipped with everything except a proprietor. Niles Dowdall—assuming that the name on the store was that of the little fat man—was evidently hiding out somewhere in the back of the building.

Don grinned to himself, and decided to give Dowdall a few minutes to make an appearance. While he waited, he crossed over to the stack of grain and held out his hand toward the cat. He was not sure how it would respond. It opened its eyes, yawned, arched its back, and then began purring loudly as Don rubbed beneath its chin. At least one resident of this town of Paradise felt friendly toward him.

Minutes passed without the return of the merchant. Don crossed to a door at the back of the room, and knocked. When there was no response, he opened the door and saw that it led to a storeroom. Another door at the back of the storeroom opened onto a cluttered back yard. It was plain that this was the way by which Dowdall had left.

Beginning to get angry, Don shut the storeroom door and looked around at the shelves. Almost everything he needed was in plain sight and readily accessible. But suppose this were a trap. Suppose Culver had instructed Dowdall what to do in case Don came to the store for supplies. If someone were to walk in and find him helping himself, how could he prove that he intended to pay?

Don crossed the front room and went out on the sidewalk. No one was in sight, but the saloon batwings were swinging gently, as though somebody had just stepped inside. Don reached the saloon door in half a dozen steps and looked in. Except for the bartender, who was polishing the mirrors, the place was empty.

Fully convinced now, that something was up, Don went a few yards farther and looked into the sheriff's office.

Sheriff Yankton was behind the desk, and his eyes regarded Don with disfavor.

"Yeah, Harding? What do you want?"

"I'd like to report a missing person," Don said. "I suppose things like that are part of your job, aren't they?"

"Missing person?" the sheriff grunted. "Who's missing?"

"The storekeeper." Without waiting for the sheriff to ask for details, Don started back toward the store, gambling on the probability that Yankton's curiosity would outweigh his reluctance to cooperate. As he had surmised, the sheriff followed him into the store.

"I saw Dowdall come in, Sheriff, but when I got here, he was gone."

The sheriff's face darkened.

"You mean you dragged me over here just on account of that? Hell, Dowdall's probably just gone to the privvy. What're you up to, Harding?"

"Me? I'm not up to anything. I just told you about a missing person. Nobody made you come over here." While Don had been talking, he had also been gathering together the things he needed at the ranch. Now he said reasonably, "Of course, as long as you're here, you can take the money for these supplies, and give it to Dowdall when he shows up. I don't imagine he'd want a stranger poking around in his merchandise, but with the sheriff as a witness..."

Yankton swore, and threw open the door to the storeroom. "Dowdall!" he yelled. "Come on in here." He returned to the front of the room and looked at Don balefully.

"You're too damned smart for your own good, Harding. One of these times . . ." He broke off and whirled on Dowdall, who had come in furtively through the back door.

"Take this man's money so he can be on his way, damn it. Where the blazes were you, anyhow?"

"Out back," Dowdall said uneasily. "Mr. Culver told me..."

Don wanted to hear what it was that Culver had said, but the sheriff cut in sharply, "Never mind. Now that you're here, wait on him." He glowered at Don. "Any other cute tricks you want to pull, Harding?"

"No," Don told him. "I'm obliged to you for your help." He turned so as to face the sheriff directly, and let his hands fall casually to his sides.

"There *is* one more thing, Sheriff. I understand you've been taking care of my brother's bay horse since the day you let them—since the day he was murdered. I'll settle up for his feed bill now, and use him to haul this stuff back to the ranch."

For a second it seemed that the sheriff would go for his gun. His jaw muscles knotted, and his right hand moved toward his holster. Then some measure of caution returned, possibly a recollection of what had happened the last time he had tried to outdraw Don. He said hoarsely, "Sure, Harding; take him any time you feel like it. He's in a shed out back. I'll get him for you."

"I'd appreciate it," Don said. He turned his back deliberately, and began throwing the supplies into a gunny sack. In a moment the door banged as the sheriff stepped out onto the street.

Later, as Don rode out of town leading Sammy's bay, he wished he had taken time to drop by and say hello to Helen Sprecher. He didn't risk going back, however. He had already stretched his luck far enough for one day.

CHAPTER EIGHT

MINNIE CULVER HAD been watching from her window and had seen her sister drive out of the ranch yard as though intending to go to town. She had wondered absently why Claire had cut short her ride and come back for the buggy, but by the time the rig was out of sight, she had quit thinking about it. After all, it really didn't make any difference what Claire did. Or what anyone else did, for that matter. All that counted was that she was going to have a baby.

In spite of her frequent crying spells, and the way she had stayed in this room to avoid being seen, Minnie wasn't as unhappy over the prospect as she let folks believe. After the baby came, at least she wouldn't be lonely any more.

Probably Pa wouldn't believe that anyone could be lonely while living in the same house with him and Claire and the Mexican servants, and with from five to fifteen cowboys on the place, depending on the season of the year. In truth, however, Minnie had never felt as though she were one of the family. She and Claire were so completely unlike that they had never been companionable. Not that Minnie disliked her sister; in fact, she was a little envious of Claire's supreme self-confidence—of her dazzling good looks, too, which she knew how to use to the greatest advantage.

As for Pa, he had always seemed a little ashamed of having fathered a daughter who preferred Homer to horses. Sometimes, when she surprised him looking at her, he reminded her of a mother hen into whose brood someone had slipped an orphaned duck.

Of course, if her mother had lived, things might have been different. From what Minnie had heard, her mother had been more like she was. But her mother had died when

60

Minnie was born, so there had never been anyone to confide in. Even the other children with whom she had attended school in Paradise had remained comparative strangers, unable to overlook the fact that she was Cletus Culver's daughter. A more aggressive girl might have known how to handle it, the way Claire had, but not Minnie. When the other girls had stayed to play together after school, and to share the secrets connected with changing from gawky adolescence to proud-breasted young womanhood, Minnie had gone home to her room, with only her books and her mirror for company.

She got up and crossed to the mirror now, her mouth pulling into an unhappy pout at sight of her ungainly figure. It was strange how little it took to change your whole life. If she hadn't become so bored with her own company that even her books couldn't hold her attention, if curiosity hadn't prompted her to go where she had no business being. . .

But it had, and now it was too late to change anything. She was going to have a baby, as a result, and, Sammy Harding was dead. Telling the truth now about how it happened wouldn't alter the facts. As she did so often lately, she began to weep. She didn't stop until she heard the buggy come back into the yard. Then, she moved languidly over to the window in time to see Claire jump out of the buggy and walk angrily toward the house, without so much as a backward glance at Whitey Larson, who had ridden in behind her.

Cletus Culver was also watching the yard, from the window in the living room. Claire's expression warned him what to expect, and he braced himself for her entrance.

She came into the room like a bronc out of a shute, saw him standing there with a cigar clamped in his teeth, and said fiercely, "This tops everything you've ever done. What was the idea sending for me as if I were a child? Don't you think I have sense enough to go to town alone when I want to?"

"When it comes to some things, you haven't sense enough to blow your nose," Culver said bluntly, talking around the cigar. When she would have retorted, he made an angry gesture. "Keep still until I'm through. In the first place, we both know you weren't just going to town; you planned it so as to get there the same time Harding did. When you spotted him riding the ridge, you . . ."

"How in the world did you know that?" she demanded. "Have you had someone spying on me?"

"You're damned right I have. After what you said about Harding the other night, I ain't taking any chances. It's bad enough having one of my daughters in trouble, but at least folks realize that Minnie couldn't help herself."

"Are you sure about that?" Claire asked pointedly.

Culver's face flushed, but he chose to ignore the question.

"Harding won't be around very long, but while he is, you're going to stay away from him. Is that clear?"

Instead of answering, Claire said curiously, "You say he won't be around. Does that mean you already have a plan for getting rid of him?"

"If you mean will I run him out at the point of a gun, the answer is no. I won't have to. Those folks in town don't want him around any more than I do. Huddleson claims he tried to scare him off by having a rattlesnake tossed into his room, but it turned out that Huddleson was the only one scared. He thinks the snake's still in the hotel. More likely the feller he hired never even had one."

"You're not hoping to scare him off with snakes?" Claire scoffed.

"Of course not. That was just Huddleson's fool idea. But when Harding finds out he can't buy supplies in town, he'll begin to see what he's up against."

"And when he does, I suppose you'll offer to buy his place for half what it's worth."

"No," Culver said. "For a fourth." He had the feeling that this conversation was getting away from him. Taking the cigar from his mouth and pointing it like a gun, he said harshly, "Never mind how I'm going to get rid of him. Just stay away from him. That's all."

"I'll think about it," she said carelessly and added, with a malicious grin, "As to his not getting supplies, he was on his way to town not an hour ago. Probably that was what he was after."

"He won't get any," Culver said with assurance.

"Would you like to bet on that?"

Without waiting for an answer, Claire left the room.

Culver scowled at her back. To tell the truth, he wouldn't have cared to put much money on it. That affair in the cafe still lay heavily on his mind. Harding wasn't a man you could push around. But he wouldn't be the first tough hombre to be brought to his knees. Perhaps it was time to start working on it. Culver threw the frayed cigar butt into the fireplace, and left the house.

He found Whitey Larson in the barn, unharnessing the team. Larson didn't notice him at first, and Culver studied him for several seconds, trying to read his expression. There had been a change in the foreman lately. Nothing you could put your finger on—he just seemed more withdrawn than in the past, as though he were harboring some secret emotion behind his impassive exterior.

Culver considered himself a good judge of men. He had to be, to have come as far as he had. It irritated him not to be able to fathom Larson's thoughts, but he was hesitant to come right out and ask for an explanation. The relationship between him and Larson was strictly that of employer and employee, which was the way Culver wanted it. Start getting friendly with one of your hired hands and you'd be asking for trouble. Larson was a capable foreman whom the men respected, and he followed orders without asking questions. When the necessity arose, he was a good man with a gun. Those were the things that counted. If he had any personal problems, that was his worry.

Larson glanced around, and for a fraction of a second, before he realized that he was not alone, his pale-blue eyes revealed something which rekindled Culver's uncertainty. Then the curtain dropped, and he said mildly, "Is there something you want, Mr. Culver?"

"There is," Culver said bluntly. "Claire tells me that Harding rode into town a short time ago. Chances are he was after supplies. I've warned the merchants not to do business with him but he's just smart enough to figure some way around it. I want you to ride over to where you can see him when he goes back to the ranch."

"And if I find that he's carrying supplies?"

"If he is, throw a scare into him."

Larson looked at him for a moment, then said soberly, "If you don't mind my saying so, I think there's a chance we'd be making a mistake. Harding can't do you any harm; his place is too small. Even if. . ."

Culver's jaw shot out, and he said savagely, "What's the matter, Larson? Has Harding got you buffaloed?"

The foreman's eyes turned hard, and his mouth became a thin line.

"Maybe I misunderstood you, Mr. Culver. Would you mind saying that again?"

"Oh, hell, don't be so quick to get your back up. I didn't mean you were scared of him."

"My mistake," Larson said softly. "I *thought* I didn't hear you right." His mouth lost some of its hardness, but there was no change in the eyes which regarded Culver. "I take it you can't accept my ideas about Harding?"

Culver shook his head angrily. This was the closest Larson had ever come to questioning one of his orders, and he had the uncomfortable feeling of having come out the loser in the exchange. In an effort to recover the advantage, he said shortly, "I wasn't asking for suggestions; I was telling you what to do. Any time you can't see your way clear to follow orders, you're free to quit."

For a moment, he thought Larson was going to take him up on it and he was too wrathful to care. Then there was a subtle change in the foreman's expression, and he said easily, "Just a case of misunderstanding, Mr. Culver. I've no complaints to offer." He took off his hat, and ran his fingers through his sun-bleached hair. "All you want me to do is find out if Harding succeeded in getting supplies, and, if he did, let him know he's in for trouble. Is that it?"

"That's it. And you'd better hurry. Harding doesn't seem to be one to waste much time."

Culver started to turn, then thought of something else. "By the way, Claire seemed pretty upset when she came in. What happened out there on the road?"

"Nothing. I just delivered your message, and she came back."

Culver glanced at the welt on Larson's cheek, and waited for some amplification of his terse explanation. When none came, he left the barn, his expression grim. There were too many undercurrents around here lately: Minnie's condition, Claire's increasingly rebellious attitude, and now this business with Whitey Larson. Somehow, they all seemed to stem from the arrival of the Hardings in the area. Thank God one of them wouldn't cause any more trouble! It would be nice if something could happen to the other one without its being tied to Box C. But, as Harding had pointed out, it would be a long time before the townsmen would undertake another lynching.

Whitey Larson came out of the barn and swung his horse toward H Bar H. Culver stood on the veranda and watched him ride out of sight. Maybe Larson's warning would do the trick. If it didn't, there were other ways—ways which had worked before and which would work again.

Don had chosen to return to H Bar H by way of the road. He kept the sorrel moving briskly, and looked back from time to time to make sure that Sammy's bay was having no difficulty—also to see if anyone was following.

It was close to noon when he entered the clearing. Red Marlowe was not in sight, but a pile of reasonably straight, pine limbs testified to his having been busy. Don swung out of his saddle, and was in the process of untying the lead rope of Sammy's bay, when he heard a horse splashing across the stream. He assumed it was Red Marlowe returning, nevertheless he had a hand on his pistol when the rider came into sight and proved to be the Box C foreman.

Instantly on guard, Don would have drawn his gun, but Larson raised his right hand shoulder high, and said calmly, "Take it easy, Harding. I'm not wearing my war paint."

Don left his pistol in its holster, but he took the precaution of moving so that his back was toward the unfinished cabin. This seemed to provide Larson with a certain amount of amusement, but, instead of mentioning it, he merely said, "I'm glad it was you that was here, instead of that redheaded kid. He'd likely have started throwing lead without giving me time to parley."

"I take it you've been here before," Don commented, "seeing you know Red Marlowe."

"You're right about my being here, but that isn't where we met. Mr. Culver and I caught him on the Box C land, pushing a handful of steers toward this valley."

"H Bar H steers," Don said pointedly.

"So we found out, but not before things almost reached the shooting stage." He grinned. "That boy's just like the rest of the redheads. He acts first and thinks afterward."

"Your boss isn't such a slouch, either, when it comes to going off half-cocked. However, I doubt that you came over here to talk about Red Marlowe's disposition."

"That's a fact, Harding. To tell the truth"—Larson's grin broadened—"to tell the truth, I'm here to let you know that if you decide to stay, you're in for trouble. Can I go back and say that I succeeded?"

Don found himself liking the Box C foreman, in spite of their being on opposite sides of the fence. He nodded, and said agreeably, "Sure. You can tell Culver I'm scared half to death. In fact, you can tell him I'm so scared I can't stop shaking long enough to saddle a horse and ride out."

"I had an idea you'd look at it that way," Larson said. He glanced at the gunny sack tied to the bay's saddle. "By the way, I take it you had no trouble buying supplies."

"None to speak of. Dowdall was a little hard to find at first, but the sheriff gave me a hand." Don grinned, and nodded toward the bay. "That sheriff's an accommodating cuss, anyway. He took care of Sammy's horse all this time, and wouldn't let me pay him a cent."

"Yankton's like that," Larson agreed ironically. "Always putting himself out for his friends."

"So I gathered," Don said, and added, "Now that you've delivered your message, would you like to get down and rest your saddle?"

"I reckon not, Harding. Chances are I might have to kill you before this is over, and it always bothers me· to kill a friend. We'd better stay enemies."

"You've got a point there," Don admitted. "But why should you and I have to fight each other in the first place? I'm not bothering anyone. All I intend to do is put this ranch into shape so that I can make it pay."

"Some folks bother mighty easy," Larson said. "My boss happens to be one of them."

"Why don't you quit? You know damned well he's in the wrong, and there must be other jobs just as good."

"I've thought of it once or twice," Larson conceded, "but

I reckon not. Culver ain't bad to work for, and the pay's good."

"Besides which," Don said quietly, "you happen to be in love with one of his daughters. Isn't that the real reason?"

Larson's grin vanished, and his eyes turned cold.

"Now you're talking about things that're none of your business, mister. Besides which, you're wrong as hell. Didn't you see what happened this morning out on the road?"

"You're right," Don said. "I apologize." But Larson's reaction had convinced him of the correctness of his guess.

"I accept your apology, Harding. You just made a mistake." Larson gathered up his reins. "Only, here's something you'd better keep in mind. I've got nothing against you personally, but if it comes to trouble between you and Mr. Culver, it's his wages I'm taking. The next time we meet, don't count on anything."

Don nodded, and watched Larson push through the brush which bordered the creek. Water splashed, and a few minutes later he came into sight on the far slope. Don watched until he was almost out of sight. As he started to move away from the cabin, something jabbed him in the back, and there was the familiar sound of a pistol being cocked.

Don froze, realizing the hopelessness of trying for the gun. It came to him then that this might explain Whitey Larson's ostensibly friendly visit. While Larson had held his interest, someone else . . .

His speculations were cut short when a voice behind him said disgustedly, "Just plain damned careless, that's what you are. A full grown man without brains enough not to put his back to an open door without finding out what's behind him!" The pistol was removed from Don's back, and the Kelso Kid shuffled into sight and looked up at him sourly. "You young fellers nowadays are lucky to stay alive long enough to start wearing long pants. When I was your age. . ."

Relieved, but also exasperated, Don said sharply, "If you're so blamed old, don't you think it'd be smart to quit fooling around with loaded guns? You're liable to get hurt."

"I suppose you're right," the Kelso Kid admitted glumly. He shoved the old pistol into its shabby holster. "There was a time when I could handle a hogleg pretty good. Maybe you won't believe it, but I used to be able to toss a dollar in

the air and drive a bullet into it before it hit the ground."
He dug around in his pocket, and—to Don's surprise, for the
Kid didn't look that prosperous—came up with a silver dollar. "Like this," he added, and flipped the silver cartwheel
toward the sky. His right hand made a blurred movement,
and the pistol appeared as if by magic. Flame blossomed
from the muzzle, and the dollar bounced in the air.

The Kelso Kid holstered his gun, and shook his head
sadly. "That's the way I used to do it when I was your age.
Nowadays I'm just too danged old and good-for-nothing."

Don gulped, and opened his mouth to say something, then
realized that he had nothing to say. He moved past the
horses, which were nervous on account of the noise, and bent
down to pick up the dollar. After rubbing his finger across
the round dent, he reached into his pocket and found another
one which he handed to the Kelso Kid.

"I'll keep yours, if it's all the same to you," he said
respectfully. "Sort of a reminder, so I won't make a fool
of myself quite so quick the next time."

"Suit yourself," the Kelso Kid said, and began scratching his chest.

Don grinned, and untied the gunny sack from the bay's
saddle. After taking it into the cabin, he returned and said,
"I don't suppose you know where Red Marlowe is?"

The Kelso Kid hesitated a moment, then said crossly,
"Now how the hell do you expect me to know that? I ain't
wet-nursin' the damned fool."

It seemed like an odd way of putting it, but it was obviously all he intended to say on the subject. When Don
came back from picketing the bay, he was gone.

CHAPTER NINE

THE AFTERNOON WAS half gone when Red
Marlowe rode in from the north, looking as though he were

a little uncertain of his reception. By then, Don had finished
trimming the pine branches, and was in the process of notch-
ing them for the roof. He leaned the ax against the cabin
and waited for what Red had to say.

"Reckon you was beginning to think I'd lit out," the boy
said. "What really happened, I thought I was on the trail of
some of those missing cows." He took off his shapeless hat
and let the breeze ruffle his red hair. "You see, I got as far
along as I could with those branches—nobody ever showed
me how to make a roof—so I thought while I was waiting
for you to come back. . ."

"You don't have to account for every minute of your
time," Don said quietly. "Just tell me about the cows."

"Yes, sir. Well I got to thinking about how many H Bar
H critters have disappeared and I decided I'd do a little
scouting around. Do you remember that barranca about a
mile north of here, the one where lightning killed a tree?"

"No, but go on."

"Well, it struck me that some of 'em might've blundered
in there in the dark, and couldn't get out."

"And had they?"

"No, sir, but a little farther up, there was the tracks of
three cows crossing over onto Box C." Red looked at Don
solemnly. "Three sets of cow tracks, and the prints of a
shod horse. I followed 'em across the ridge."

"Pretty risky," Don said. "Next time you'd better wait
until you aren't alone."

"Yes, sir, but all I could think of at the time was maybe
finding out what's been going on."

"And what *did* you find out?"

"I didn't find the cows, if that's what you're wondering,
but I trailed 'em far enough to know they was being driven
toward Culver's headquarters. You know something? I bet
those Box C punchers have been eating H Bar H beef."
Red's face knotted with anger. "If we was both to ride over
there right now, chances are we could. . ."

"No," Don said, controlling his own temper with difficulty, "Not now. Not until we finish what we're doing.
It might just be a trick to toll us away, so they could wreck
what we've already done."

"Well, you're the boss," Red said, his tone indicating disappointment.

Don nodded, and went back to work. Red rode the pinto out of the clearing. When he came back, it was evident that something had boosted his spirits. He grinned at Don and said admiringly, "Why didn't you say you'd got Sammy's horse back? Did you have any trouble?"

"None to speak of. I wouldn't go so far as to say that the sheriff was happy about it." Don matched Red's grin, and motioned toward one of the pine boughs. "Grab hold of the other end, and we'll get started on the roof. If you don't know how it's done, it's time you learned. One of these days you'll be wanting to build a place for yourself, and start raising a bunch of redheads."

"Not me," Red said positively. "I ain't ever going to get married." He grinned a little sheepishly. "Tell you the truth, Don, I'm scared to death of girls. They make me feel like a fool."

"You'll get over it," Don laughed. "Or at least used to it. One of these days. . ."

"No, sir. Not me." He reached for one of the limbs.

Even with both of them working, putting up the roof was a hard job. Since the fireplace was in the center of one wall, and the door was directly opposite, Don's plan called for a ridgepole running crossways of the building, with the roof sloping down toward front and back. Each end of the ridgepole would be supported by a stout timber erected inside the cabin, its base resting on the dirt. A straight pole ten feet long was laid in notches at the tops of the two supports, allowing an overhang of six inches at each end, then two shorter branches slanted down from each end of the ridgepole to the corners of the cabin.

With this as a skeleton, they placed poles parallel to the ridge and about a foot apart. Since there was neither the equipment nor the time to manufacture shakes, they laid a solid covering of small poles at right angles to those, with their upper ends nailed to the ridge, and their lower extremities resting on the top logs of the cabin's front and back walls. Due to the crookedness of the limbs, there were innumerable gaps, but these would be taken care of later.

It wasn't a job to be done in a hurry, but by dusk of the

following day it was finished, including the cutting and erection of logs to form the ends of the gables, and the stringing of pine boughs to make it rain-proof.

They celebrated by eating supper in the cabin, although there was yet no furniture, and they had to sit on the ground. While they were eating, the Kelso Kid hailed them from the edge of the clearing. Don called to him to come on in, and presently he did, riding a hammer-headed claybank which looked about as weather-beaten as its owner. Remembering how badly he had underestimated the Kelso Kid, Don postponed judgment on the horse.

"Figured you fellers'd be about done," the Kelso Kid said, squinting at the cabin in the fading daylight. "Not bad, for a couple of greenhorns."

"Figured, hell!" Don said, grinning. "It's a funny thing, you showing up just when the work's over. I'd bet even money you've been watching us all the time."

"You'd win," the Kelso Kid admitted cheerfully. "I already told you how I feel about work. Besides that, I'm scared of it. You want to know why?"

"I'm sure it'll be worth listening to," Don said. "Let's hear it."

"Go ahead, laugh if you want to, but this is gospel truth. Used to be I was as hard-working a fool as anybody. Then one day I got to meditatin' on it, and I saw the light." He paused long enough to get out of the saddle and drop his reins.

"Yes, sir, I got to thinkin', and it come to me. Paw was a hard workin' son-of-a-gun, like his paw before him. Fact is, everybody in my family was a regular doggoned beaver, and you know something? Every one of 'em's dead." He looked at Don guilelessly. "A feller would be a fool to go up against odds like that. I ain't done a lick of work since."

Don laughed, and glanced around at Red to see how he was taking it. To his surprise, Red wasn't even smiling.

The Kelso Kid noticed this too, and said crossly, "What've you been feeding the redhead? green quinces?" He turned to unbuckle one of his saddlebags and held out a bottle. "Maybe this'll sweeten him up. I figured you was entitled to a wingding."

"In that case," Don said. "We forgive you." He uncorked

the bottle, took a healthy swallow, and handed it to Red, who hesitated a moment, then tilted it to his mouth before handing it back to the Kelso Kid.

"Much obliged," Red murmured, and managed a weak grin.

The Kelso Kid turned the bottle over to Don.

"You keep it, Harding. I ain't tasted the stuff for years. In my business, I don't dare."

Don remembered the Kelso Kid's skill with a gun, and let it ride. He motioned toward the cabin door, and said, "Come on in. There's no extra charge."

"Figured I would," the Kelso Kid said. He stopped to examine the door, which Don had made by nailing split logs to a pole frame, the whole affair hanging on iron hinges which he had brought back from town. With only a grunt, which might have expressed either satisfaction or disgust, the Kelso Kid went on to the middle of the room and scowled around at the flame-lit interior.

The portholes in the walls caught his interest, and he shuffled over for a better look. Without commenting, he left the cabin, returning presently with a slab of wood which Don had discarded. He tossed it into a corner, and said aggrievedly, "Them holes're all right for a six-footer, but I'll be damned if I'm going to stand on my tippytoes to shoot."

By now, Don was used to the Kelso Kid's surprises, so he didn't ask the obvious question. If the grimy little man had made up his mind that he would shoot through those holes in the walls, nobody was likely to change it. Don wasn't even sure he wanted to. Having the Kelso Kid on your side might prove to be a comfort. One thing sure, if the Kelso Kid started shooting through those portholes, it would be a lot better to have him on the inside aiming out, than on the outside aiming in.

His inspection over, the Kelso Kid sat down with his back against a wall, and said querulously, "Ain't you going to ask me what's new since you've been building this shack?"

"Sure," Don said obligingly, "what's new since we've been building this shack?"

"Well, for one thing. . ." He shoved his hands inside his shirt and began scratching himself, a procedure which seemed habitual with him. "For one thing Seth Huddleson had every stick of furniture moved out of the hotel. Seems he thought there was a rattlesnake in the place. Figure that one out if you can."

Don smiled, but didn't say anything.

"Also, Sheriff Yankton's been spreading it around that you beat him out of the feed bill on your brother's horse."

"Yankton's a liar."

"We're supposed to be talking about what's new," the Kelso Kid reminded him. "Yankton's been a liar all his life. However, he claims he's going to toss you in the hoosegow next time he catches you in Paradise."

"What's to stop him from coming out here after me?" Don asked. "Isn't this ranch on his territory?"

"If it ain't, it will be when he wants it to, which will be whenever Cletus Culver gives him the nod."

"Then you think Yankton takes orders from Culver?"

"Don't everybody?" the Kelso Kid asked. "Well, maybe not quite, at that. Will Tully's his own man, and that gal—" He broke off abruptly, and got to his feet. "Hell, I almost forgot. The gal that runs the cafe sent you something. I'll get it."

As soon as he was out of the cabin, Red Marlowe said uneasily, "What was his idea bringing that piece of wood in here? Did you ask him to throw in with us or something?"

"No, but it strikes me that the Kelso Kid does about as he pleases, without waiting to be asked. Why? Is something bothering you?"

"I don't like him," Red said tensely. "How do we know he ain't working against us? Maybe being paid by old man Culver, or something."

"We don't," Don acknowledged, and added reasonably, "For that matter, how do you and I know we can trust each other?" He smiled, and reached out to slap the boy on the shoulder. "Don't worry so much, Red. We can keep our eyes open."

There wasn't time to say more, as the Kelso Kid came back into the cabin. He was carrying his saddlebags in one hand, and a rifle in the other. After leaning the rifle against the wall, he unfastened the flap of the saddlebag, and took out a newspaper-wrapped bundle, which he handed to Don. Curiously, Don knelt down in front of the fire and unfolded the paper. He began to chuckle as a pie came into sight. Behind him, the Kelso Kid said wonderingly, "Man, you must be a fast worker. I've been eating in that place off and on for a year, and she never gave me any free grub."

"Can I help it if I'm a natural-born lady-killer?" Don inquired. "Of course, if it worries you, you two don't have to help me eat it."

"Who's worried?" Red asked, and for the first time since the Kelso Kid's arrival, he seemed pleased about something. It was really true, Don told himself, that the way to a man's heart was through his stomach. Especially a man who was little more than a boy.

"She sent something else, too," the Kelso Kid said, and pulled an envelope out of his pocket.

Don took it, and straightened up, immediately sober. If Helen Sprecher had seen fit to write him, she must have had a compelling reason. She hardly seemed the kind of girl who would indulge in frivolity.

Red Marlowe and the Kelso Kid were watching him, so he said, "Go ahead and cut it three ways. I'll be with you in a minute."

The envelope had been pasted shut with flour and water. Don broke the seal and held the letter to the light.

Dear Mr. Harding (it said). *Since you claim to be known as a hearty eater, maybe you can use this apple pie which I had planned on throwing out. If you can't, I'm sure Mr. Kelso will be glad to have it.*

You may be interested in learning that there is talk going around town linking your name with that of Claire Culver. If I may offer some advice, it is that you avoid going anywhere without a friend along as witness.

P.S. Your brother's grave marker is still standing.

Don's first reaction to what she had reported was one of anger. There wasn't much doubt in his mind as to who had started the talk. Not Culver, certainly, since it would reflect on his own family. And not Whitey Larson. A man didn't circulate rumors about the woman he loved, even if his love was undeclared and unreciprocated. Nor would any of the townsmen be back of it; they were too afraid of Cletus Culver.

This left only one likely suspect—Claire herself. From what Don had seen of her, she wouldn't hesitate to bring discredit to the Culver name, not if by doing so she could satisfy her own selfish purposes. What was that saying about a woman scorned? Most likely Claire Culver had never before gone to so much trouble to offer a man a buggy-ride. If she had, it was a pretty safe bet she hadn't been turned down.

He read the note again, and some of his bitterness drained away. It must have taken courage for a girl like Helen Sprecher, who detested violence, to risk involving herself in a controversy like this—and on the unpopular side, at that. Then there was that postscript. It had been considerate of her to reassure him about Sammy's grave.

On impulse, he turned to the Kelso Kid.

"You mentioned eating in the cafe off and on. Tell me, is there a man connected with it in some way, or doesn't that name on the front mean anything?"

"N. Napoleon, you mean?" The Kelso Kid shook his head. "He's been dead for years." He licked the pie off his fingers, and went on.

"The gal that sent you this pie—she's nobody's fool. With trail crews coming through here every spring and fall, she figured a single gal running a cafe wouldn't have a chance. That name fools strangers into thinking there's a man in the back room. She ain't dumb, anyway. The way I hear it, she was teaching school back east somewhere, and some feller that was supposed to be a big mucky-muck in the town, the mayor or something, figured his job entitled him to special privileges with the school teacher. She didn't see it that way, and when he began acting like a boar hog, she opened his scalp with a stove poker. The next day she came out here and bought a cafe."

"She told you that?"

"Hell, no! Some hardware salesman from back east recognized her and told us about it." The Kelso Kid looked at Don speculatively. "How come you're so interested in the gal? You figuring on marrying her or something?"

"Good Lord, no! I've got troubles enough, without having

a wife." He grinned. "Besides, she doesn't strike me as
the marrying sort. More likely she'll end up an old maid."

"Don't let that prim get-up fool you," the Kelso Kid
cautioned. "Women and horses have one thing in common;
you can't tell from their riggin' what's inside. Did you happen to notice that jughead I rode in on?"

Don nodded.

"Pretty sorry looking old bag of bones, ain't he? Tomorrow morning, suppose you see how he rides."

"No, thanks," Don said, and took the dented dollar out
of his pocket. "Anyway, I didn't mean it as anything against
the girl. If I wanted a wife, likely I could do worse. It's
just that I'm not interested."

"Then why'd you ask?" the Kelso Kid grumbled. "You
think I've got nothing to do but answer damfool questions?"
He picked up his rifle and stomped out of the cabin.

Red Marlowe pointed at the dollar.

"What happened to that?"

"Looks like somebody's been using it for a target," Don
said innocently. "I picked it up in the clearing."

"Can I see it a minute?"

Don handed it to him, and Red rubbed a finger over the
indentation.

"I remember seeing one like this once before. Some gun
salesman tossed it up and hit it in the air. That's why
the bullet didn't go clean through, because there was nothing to back it up." He looked at Don accusingly. "Did you
do this yourself?"

"Not me," Don said, shaking his head. "If that's the way
this got dented, it was done by a better shot than I am." He
took back the dollar and dropped it into his pocket. "Now,
I'll see how this pie tastes, before you two starved dogies
finish it up."

The pie was even better than he had hoped, in spite of
its having been in the Kelso Kid's saddlebags a considerable
time. While Don was still eating, the Kelso Kid sauntered
back into the cabin, this time carrying his blanket roll
under his arm, and his saddle over his shoulder. He de-
bated a moment, then dropped the saddle in one of the
corners farthest from the fireplace.

"I'll sleep here. You fellers can take your pick of the rest."

Red Marlowe looked as though he were about to explode, but it struck Don as funny.

"I take it you're moving in. Is that the general idea?"

"Of course I am. I can't leave you two babes-in-the-woods without any protection." He unfastened his blanket roll, flipped it on the ground, and sprawled on his back, using the saddle as a pillow. "Another thing; we're going to have to stand guard. You," he pointed at Red Marlowe. "You take the first watch. At ten o'clock."

"Whoa!" Don said, still smiling. "Maybe we'd better get something straight right now. Like you said when you first showed up, you're pretty as hell, but that doesn't mean you're going to rule the roost. We'll put up with you the best we can, so long as you don't snore. In fact, we'll even let you snore a little, unless you overdo it, but when it comes to giving orders, I'll be the one to say what's what. Comprende?"

"Si," the Kelso Kid said. "I get it, all right." His voice was as gruff as ever, but Don thought he detected a twinkle in his eyes. "One thing I'll say for you Harding. It don't take you long to figure out who's boss." He turned toward the wall, and ten minutes later was asleep.

CHAPTER TEN

HELEN SPRECHER HAD argued with herself at length before sending the message to Don Harding. As a matter of principle, she didn't get involved in the town's controversies, although there were plenty of times when she had had to bite her tongue to keep from speaking out. Of course, the prime example of this had been the lynching of Sammy Harding. She would have broken her rule then, but by the time she had heard about it, it had been too late to do any good. When a group of normally law-abiding men become infected with mob spirit, nothing will stop them except a blast from a shotgun, certainly not the pleas of a girl.

Still—and it was this which had tormented her ever since that horrible day—she couldn't help feeling that there must have been a time at which she *could* have prevented it. There must have been a beginning; someone must have uttered the word which started it off. Perhaps if she been more alert . . .

These thoughts had returned time after time to bother her. Now, they were on her mind again, as she started getting ready for bed. If only she had snuffed out the first spark before it had turned into a conflagration. If . . .

She was standing before the mirror in her little bedroom behind the restaurant, loosening the bun at the back of her neck. As she removed the last pin, her dark hair cascaded around her shoulders. She picked up a hairbrush and began brushing it automatically, entirely oblivious to the change it made in her looks.

Vanity was not one of Helen's traits. She was inclined to take herself pretty much for granted. In fact, until that unfortunate incident back east, she had never thought of herself as having physical qualifications which would arouse a man's passion. Nor had she supposed that her own passions, though of a different nature, would have permitted her to get so much satisfaction out of banging a man over the head with a poker. It still embarrassed her that she should look back on it with secret pleasure.

Afterwards, she had decided that it might have been partly her own fault. It had happened in the Spring, when men's natures were said to be most ardent, and she had had been wearing a rather low-necked, clingy type of dress, instead of the more sedate garb considered appropriate for school teachers. Still, she hadn't dreamed that just looking at a little bare skin would make a man lose his head. Even now, she didn't see why it had made so much difference.

Curious, she laid down the hairbrush and leaned closer to the mirror for a more detailed study of her reflection. Considering it objectively, she supposed she might be considered not unattractive. Her features were regular and not out of proportion. Against the dark frame of her hair, which, now that it had been brushed, was the color of burnished mahogany, she guessed her face might even be considered pretty.

On impulse she unfastened her wrapper and let it fall to the floor. The mirror was only large enough to picture her from the waist up, but what she saw wasn't unpleasing; firm breasts, and soft skin the color of rich milk. It came to her with considerable surprise that below the neck she didn't look so terribly different from those posters that she had seen tacked up in the railroad depot in Kansas City. Good heavens, what would her customers think if they were to see her the way she looked now? What would Don Harding...?

For some inexplicable reason, her reflection turned a sudden pink. She hurriedly looked away, grabbed up a nightgown, pulled it over her head, and buttoned it to the neck. Without another glance at the mirror, she blew out the lamp and scrambled into bed.

Three hours later, she was still awake, staring up at the ceiling. From far off came the faint sound of what could have been a gunshot. It was followed quickly by several more so close together that Helen couldn't count them. She sat up in bed, pulled aside the window curtain, and looked out at the starlit sky. Somewhere in town a dog howled, but there was no more shooting. She got up and opened the window, hoping for some clue as to what had happened. All she heard was the wheeze of an accordion over at Ruby Salmon's Palace of Venus. She closed the window and slipped back into bed, telling herself that the source of the shots might have been in almost any direction, the way sounds carried in this country. It just happened that her window faced the north. Probably that was why she had thought they were out toward Don Harding's place. Chances were he hadn't even heard them.

In this, she was wrong. Don heard the shots; in fact, they woke him out of a sound sleep. After the first one, he lay motionless waiting for a hint as to what was going on. Then the gun roared again, this time letting go with wild abandon. Don rolled to his feet, grabbing his gun in the same motion, and headed for the door; he noticed automatically that the Kelso Kid had come off the floor and snatched up his rifle.

As Don burst into the open, he heard horses galloping. Then Red Marlowe, who had been on guard duty, yelled frantically, "Good God! I've been shot!"

Don ran toward the sound of Red's voice, cursing himself for having placed the boy in a position of danger. He saw Red standing spread-legged at the edge of the clearing, his face looking ghastly in the starlight.

"Take it easy," Don cautioned, afraid Red might mistake him for an enemy.

"Yes, sir," Red said, his voice a little less wild. "Damn their guts, they was right on top of me before I saw 'em. They..."

"Never mind, fella; the first thing we have to do is see how bad you're hurt. You can tell us the rest of it later." Don reached for the boy's rifle, then took hold of an arm. "Can you walk?"

"I reckon," Red said. "Likely I ain't hurt so bad as I thought. It's just that I've never been shot before, and it scared me." He took a tentative step, then hobbled toward the cabin, favoring his left leg. Don followed him in, and closed the door.

"Where's Kelso?" Red demanded. "By God, I bet he's the..."

"Simmer down, Red. Kelso was in his blankets when the shooting started. Maybe he's out scouting around." Don picked up some twigs and tossed them on the still-smoldering embers. They smoked a minute, then burst into flame. "Now let's have a look at that leg."

Red unfastened his belt, and lowered his pants to his knees, revealing skinnny young shanks. "Reckon I did a lot of hollering over nothing," he said apologetically.

"Let's hope so. Turn around so I can see."

Red did, and the firelight glistened on wet blood. Don touched the boy's thigh, and grunted with relief.

"You were lucky. All you got out of it is a nice white scar. That bullet could just as easy have broken a bone or cut an artery." He grinned. "Here's where we use some more of that whiskey."

While Don sterilized the gash and fashioned a dressing, Red told him what had happened.

"There was just two of 'em, near as I could make out. I spotted the first one fooling around with our horses. When I yelled for him to put up his hands, the other one opened up from the dark. I emptied my gun at him, and by that time the first one was gone with our horses."

"Do you think you hit anyone?"

"Most likely I didn't," Red said ruefully. "With that bullet in my leg, and everything, I wasn't aiming so careful. I'm sorry."

"Forget it, boy. Being shot at is something that takes a good deal of getting used to. I'm just thankful you're all right."

"Ain't we goin' after them?"

"On foot, and in the dark?" Don grinned wryly. "We'll wait till morning, when we'll be able to see their tracks. In the meantime, you'd better get some sleep. I'll stay awake in case anything happens."

"What about *him?*" Red asked, pointing at the Kelso Kid's blankets.

"Oh, he'll come back when he feels like it. He always does."

It was over an hour before the Kelso Kid showed up, riding bareback on the claybank, and leading the other three horses by their tie-ropes. By then, Red Marlowe was sleeping as though drugged, probably because he had lost some blood. Don left the cabin, closing the door quietly after him. A full moon had come up, and it was light enough for him to see the quizzical expression on the Kelso Kid's face.

"Something wrong in there, Harding?"

"Just that I don't want to wake up Red if I can help it. He got creased by a bullet, and lost a little blood. It won't hurt for him to get some sleep." He moved over to take the ropes. "What did you do? catch up with 'em on foot and knock 'em out of their saddles?"

"On foot, hell!" the Kelso Kid snorted. "They only got these other three nags. This old jughead of mine wasn't even tied. I've got him trained to hang around, and nobody but me can get near him. Trouble with tying a horse, you're

never sure whether you're tying him for yourself or someone else."

This sounded sensible, Don thought, provided you knew
how to make a horse stay around. He let it pass, and said,
"That accounts for the one you're riding, but how'd you
get the other three?"

"Picked 'em up about a mile away. I guess when Marlowe
got buck fever and emptied his gun at the sky, them fellers
decided their hides was more important than a few broncs."

"Then you didn't get a look at anybody?"

"Nope. Maybe we'll be able to pick up their sign in the
morning."

"That's what I told Red," Don said. "Go back and finish your sleep, if you want to. I'll take care of the horses
and keep a lookout until morning."

"You'll be wasting your time; they won't be coming back
tonight. But I guess that's your·problem." The Kelso Kid
slipped off his horse, and it wandered off toward the creek.
"Anyhow, I'm all in favor of that part about going back
to sleep. See you in the morning."

Don watched him go into the cabin, then tied the three
horses where he could keep them in sight. Tomorrow—today,
rather, as it was well past midnight—he'd have to get busy
on some kind of shelter where they could be locked up at
night. This business of standing guard was all right for
a night or two, but not as a regular thing. In order to do a
good day's work, a man needed his sleep. And it was going to
take a lot of work to put this ranch on a profitable basis.
After all, that was what he had come here for, to operate
a ranch. He would still do it, in spite of everything.

Before dawn, a breeze sprung up out of the north, and,
by the time the sun rose, it had turned into a gale, scouring
up dust from the cleared area around the cabin, and threatening to tear loose the pine boughs which were tied to the
roof rafters. The three horses turned their rumps to the
wind, and stood with heads down, tails whipping between
their hind legs.

The Kelso Kid came out of the cabin looking no crankier
than usual. He studied the sky a moment and said positively, "It'll keep up like this till sundown, and then run out

of steam. You got to figure on one of these big blows every six months or so. We can be thankful it ain't snowing."

The cabin door opened again, and Red Marlowe came out, limping a little. His head jerked up as he saw the horses, and he looked at Don in surprise.

"What happened? Did they come drifting back?"

"Not exactly. The Kelso Kid rode out in the night and brought them in. Whoever it was that paid us a visit, evidently didn't know there were three of us here last night. Either that, or they couldn't catch the claybank. He was wandering around loose and they must've missed him."

"Pretty lucky," Red said. "I suppose now we can ride over to Box C."

Don shook his head, and the boy's chin fell.

"You mean we're going to let 'em get away with it?"

"No, but right now we're going to stay here and build a shed for the horses, so this won't happen again."

"Cripes! They'll think we're scared!"

"Let them, then," Don said. "Maybe they'll also think we're smart enough not to walk into a trap. There's no way on God's green earth we can prove who it was that shot you and made off with the horses. Not unless the horses can talk, and I know my sorrel can't. Culver warned me he'd find a way of getting me out of the country. There's nothing he'd like better than to catch me on his land, accusing him of stealing the very horse I was riding."

"Damn it, how about my leg?" Red grumbled.

"Well, how about it? Maybe I'd better have a look."

"It's all right," Red said shortly. "That ain't what I meant. Them fellers put a bullet in it, and now you say we ain't going to do anything. The way it looks to me . . ."

"Oh hell," the Kelso Kid growled. "You ain't going to cure a scratch on your leg getting a hole in your head. If you can't talk sense, why don't you keep still?"

It was the first time the Kelso Kid had really spoken out about Red Marlowe, although it had been evident from the first that he hadn't much patience where the boy was concerned. Red's cheeks flushed and he took a step toward the older man, but Don moved between them and said mildly, "Take it easy, Red. If Culver wants trouble, we'll give it

to him. It's just that we'll do it when and where we want
to, not to suit him. Doesn't that make sense?"

"I guess so," Red muttered, still looking disgruntled. He
stared at the ground a second, then met Don's eyes. "Reckon
I had no business blowing up, but when I think how close
they came to breaking my leg . . ."

"I know," Don said, "but suppose we forget it and have
some breakfast." He looked around at the Kelso Kid. "Is
that agreeable to you?"

"Sure," the Kelso Kid said, and added for Red's evident
benefit, although he directed the words at Don, "You know,
they claim the north wind makes folks jumpy." He grinned.
"Sure must be tough for anyone living at the South Pole,
where there's no other direction for it to blow."

Don chuckled, but Red Marlowe turned away without
a smile, and limped around the corner of the cabin. The
Kelso Kid watched him with an expression Don couldn't
interpret.

Breakfast helped relieve the tension; even Red Marlowe
brightened considerably after stowing away a dozen flapjacks and several thick slices of bacon. In the course of
the meal, the Kelso Kid looked at Don and said pointedly,
"By the way, you never did tell us what was in that letter
I brought."

"I didn't, did I?" Don agreed, and helped himself to
another cup of coffee.

"Hell of a note," the Kelso Kid muttered. "I break my
neck bringing it out to you, and you don't even tell me what
it said."

"I thought you were mostly interested in the pie," Don
said. "If I'd dreamed it was the letter you were worried
about, you could have had that, and Red and I would've eat-
en the pie."

"Go to hell!" the Kelso Kid said amiably. He slung his
saddle over his shoulder, picked up the rifle, and left the
cabin.

Red Marlowe waited until the Kelso Kid's footsteps were
swallowed by the wind, then said tightly, "Where do you
suppose he's going in such a hurry?"

"Hard to say," Don told him, smiling. "Most likely he

couldn't stand the idea of sitting around watching us work, so he decided to get out of sight." He noticed the boy's bitter expression, and added quietly, "It strikes me you're carrying quite a chip on your shoulder where the Kelso Kid's concerned. If you are, you'd better get rid of it. We can't afford to lose the few friends we have."

"Maybe not," Red admitted. "But I ain't so sure he *is* a friend." He heaved a troubled sigh. "On the other hand, I probably ain't been doing much myself to be proud of. If you say he's all right, it's good enough for me."

"Good," Don said, with relief. "Now let's get busy. We've got to fix a place for our horses."

"You mean a barn or something?"

Don had been giving the matter additional thought, and he shook his head.

"That'd take too long. We'll build a good stout corral, with a gate we can lock. Later, when there's more time, we can do the job right."

As the Kelso Kid had predicted, the wind kept up all day, adding to the difficulty of building the corral. However, by sundown, Don and Red had enclosed an area large enough for their immediate needs, using the back wall of the cabin for one of the sides, and setting stout posts for the other three. They hung a gate close to the corner of the cabin, and nailed peeled rails to the posts the rest of the way around the three sides. As a finishing touch, Don devised a lock which couldn't be unfastened without difficulty by anyone not familiar with it, especially not in the dark.

They turned their three horses into the corral, scrubbed up at the creek, and built a fire in the fireplace preparatory to eating supper. While they were waiting for the potatoes and bacon to fry and the coffee to boil, Red said worriedly, "Now that it's done, what's to stop 'em from burning it? We can't stay here and watch it all the time."

"That's right," Don agreed. "However, there's one point in our favor. Whoever might want to burn us out, either Culver or the men who were in that lynch mob, they've got more at stake than we have. All we can lose is the results of three or four days' work, plus a few logs. Unless they mean to wipe us out entirely, they'd have to figure on our trying to get even." He smiled grimly. "One of Culver's sheds would be worth more than this cabin, and his house, probably a hundred times as much. The same thing applies to the merchants."

"Then you think they'll leave us alone?"

"I wouldn't go that far, but I doubt if they'll be the ones to start setting fire to anything." He lifted the skillet off the fire, and scooped meat and potatoes into their tin plates, noticing as he did, that Red still looked dissatisfied.

"I've got a pretty good idea how you feel, boy. Someone's been running off our cows, and someone took a shot at you and tried to steal our horses. You're thinking we ought to do something about it, that anyone with guts would oil his shooting iron and start raising hell. When I was your age, I would've felt the same way, but I've had a little sense knocked into me in the last dozen years. I've seen too many people go off half-cocked, and afterwards wish they hadn't. When I start raising hell, I want to be sure it's against the right people."

"But it's just got to be Culver," Red protested. "Those cow tracks . . ."

"Were made by some cows being driven onto Box C land," Don finished. "Maybe Culver was in back of it, and maybe somebody just wants us to think so. He's the one who came right out and told me to leave the country, but there must be a dozen men in town who would like to see me go: the ones who helped lynch Sammy—not to mention the sheriff. I made him look sort of foolish, and he's too small a man to enjoy a joke if it's on himself."

"I guess so," Red conceded. "Just the same, though . . ." He picked up his plate and began to eat.

"Cheer up, Red," Don said. "When the time comes, there'll be plenty of hell raising, maybe enough even for you."

Red grinned weakly, and reached for the coffee pot.

While they were eating, the wind died down, leaving a strange silence and a lingering smell of dust in the air. From somewhere in the distance came the sound of a horse's hoof striking a rock, and Don rose to his feet.

"Maybe it's going to start right now," he said, and headed toward one of the portholes.

CHAPTER ELEVEN

INSTEAD OF A townsman or one of Culver's riders, it was the Kelso Kid who rode into the clearing; his claybank was easily recognizable even in the failing daylight. Don left the porthole, crossed to the doorway, and stepped outside.

"Put your horse in the corral and come on in. You're just in time to miss your supper."

"I've et," the Kelso Kid said. "What's this about a corral?"

"See for yourself. It's around here." Don circled the corner of the cabin, motioning for the mounted man to follow.

"Looks like you've been busy," the Kelso Kid said, after a brief inspection. "It's a good stout corral, but what's to keep somebody from sneaking up in the night and opening the gate?"

"Try it and see," Don invited.

The Kelso Kid started to dismount, then settled back in the saddle and shook his head.

"No, thanks, young feller. You're too blamed willing. What've you got rigged up? a shotgun on a string or something?"

"Nothing that bloodthirsty, just a lock that might give someone a little trouble. I'll open it and you can put your horse with the others."

"I reckon not. No use spoiling him." The Kelso Kid swung to the ground, uncinched his saddle, and lifted it off the horse's back. He laid it against the cabin while he slipped off the bridle, then would have picked it up except that Don beat him to it.

Red Marlowe had come as far as the cabin door. He moved aside to let them enter, and mumbled a faint "howdy" to the Kelso Kid.

87

"How's the leg, Marlowe?"

"All right," Red said. "There's a little coffee in the pot if you're thirsty."

"No, thanks," the Kelso Kid said, then, apparently realizing that the boy was trying to be friendly, added quickly, "Well, maybe I will at that. Like I was telling Harding, I've already et, but I've swallowed so much dust today, maybe a cup of coffee would wash it down." He dropped his bridle on the saddle which Don had laid down, and crossed to the fireplace to pick up the coffeepot. When he had poured a cupful and drunk it, he looked around at Don.

"Speaking of dust, that north wind blew so hard it wiped out those hoofprints like they was never there."

Red Marlowe said quickly, "Then you mean you couldn't follow them even as far as the Box C line?"

"Not much beyond the far side of the creek," the Kelso Kid acknowledged glumly.

"Damn it!" Red grumbled. "They *would* pick a time when nobody could trail 'em!"

The Kelso Kid gave him a thoughtful glance, then looked up inquisitively at Don, who said casually, "Red's all in favor of riding over to Culver's place and forcing a showdown. He's convinced they're the ones who shot him."

"And you?"

"I'm willing to admit he's probably right, but I want to be sure."

"Yeah," the Kelso Kid said. He put down his empty cup, and moved away from the fire. "Well, maybe you're smart to look at it that way. Chances are you'll be having your hands full even without Culver."

"Meaning what?"

"Meaning I've been hanging around town most of the day. That's where I et—at the cafe." He grinned. "No, she didn't send any notes, or any pie, either, but she did put me onto something. They're saying around town that you tried the same stunt with Claire Culver that your brother did with Minnie."

"That they *claim* Sammy did," Don corrected.

"All right, damn it, that they *claim* he did. Do you want to hear this, or don't you?"

"Keep talking."

"Well, according to the gossip, you waited until you saw Claire Culver driving along toward town, then rode out to stop her. If it hadn't been that Whitey Larson happened along—" He lifted his shoulders in a meaningful shrug.

"Does Larson say that's what happened?"

"I don't know. That's the trouble; nobody seems to remember who started it, but it's all over town now."

"The crazy fools! Don't they have enough sense to realize that if what they're saying was true, Larson would've called me right on the spot? The fact that Larson and I are both alive should be proof it didn't happen."

"It's pretty hard to prove anything to a bunch of fellers that don't want to be convinced," the Kelso Kid said. "Them folks in town would like to get rid of you, and they don't much care how. As long as you're here, they'll never be able to forget what they did to your brother."

"That's because they aren't sure themselves that he was guilty." Don smiled without humor, and turned toward Red Marlowe.

"You weren't here at the time they claim Sammy raped the Culver girl, but you must've come to work for him not long after. Did he ever say anything at all about her?"

Red hesitated a moment, then shook his head. "No, sir; he never even mentioned her name."

Don was bothered by that momentary hesitation.

"You make it sound as if you aren't absolutely sure. If there's something on your mind, now's the time to get it out in the open. Do you think maybe Sammy really did . . ."

"My God no!" Red protested vehemently. "What they say about him pulling her off her horse is a stinkin' lie. Sammy wouldn't do—wouldn't've done a thing like that in a thousand years." He looked quickly at the Kelso Kid, as though daring him to deny it, then back toward Don.

"You told me, if there was something on my mind to get it out in the open, so I guess that's what you meant. Sammy didn't do what they say he did, but I can't help thinking, if Minnie Culver rode out here and got to know him, and if they began getting pretty friendly—well, Sammy was pretty lonesome here all by himself, and from what I've seen of the Culvers, they're used to getting what they want."

Don was about to scoff at the idea, but he remembered

his own experience with Claire Culver. Sammy hadn't been experienced enough to contend with a designing woman. With a sinking feeling, he said quietly, "You think it might've been something the girl got herself into willingly? Is that it?"

"I'm not sure what I think," Red said miserably. "It's just that I'm trying to figure what could've happened. Minnie didn't get like she is by herself."

"I imagine we'll all agree on that," Don said dryly. "Of course, it's humanly possible you've got the right answer, but in that case, why couldn't she have told the truth? She wouldn't've been the first girl to get married with a baby already on the way."

"I can answer that," the Kelso Kid cut in. "All their lives, them two Culver gals've been brought up to think they should have anything they set their minds on. You wouldn't expect one of them to give up all that and move into a log cabin on a little shirttail spread—meaning no offense to your ranch. Likely she knew what her paw would've done if she'd admitted the truth. There'd've been a blowup you could've heard in China. Minnie would've ended up married to a boy that couldn't give her anything fancier than sidemeat and beans. The way it is, she'll have her baby in a fine bed, with Doc White standing by, and everyone feeling sorry for her."

"Maybe you're right," Don admitted. "But, as I've said before, I'd like to hear this from the girl herself." He turned abruptly and grabbed his hat off a nail.

"You ain't fixing to go see Minnie now, are you?" Red cried.

"No. I'm riding into town. Chances are those merchants aren't ready for another lynching so soon after the first one. But if someone's working on them, they may get their nerve up. I'm going to try and head it off while there's still time."

"Then I'll go with you," Red said.

"No. Somebody has to stay here."

"What's the matter with him staying?" Red demanded, looking at the Kelso Kid. "Damn it, Don, just because I got a little excited last night, don't mean I'll do it again."

"This has nothing to do with last night," Don explained

patiently, wishing that Red wasn't so quick to take offense.
"It just happens that you and I are running the ranch, and
if I can't be here, it's up to you to take over. Besides, I'm
going to ask the Kelso Kid to do something else." He
turned to face the older man.

"How do you rate with the Culvers?"

"So-so," the Kelso Kid said, shrugging. "Culver probably
don't know I'm alive. He don't bother me, and I don't
bother him. I've seen the two gals now and then, but they
haven't rolled their eyes at me or anything. Played a little
poker with Whitey Larson in the back room of the saloon
on Saturday nights. That's about it."

"Then there's no reason to think you'd be shot on sight
if you showed up at Box C?"

"Not that I know of. Why?"

"I wouldn't mind knowing what's going on over there—
whether Culver's getting ready to try running me out of the
country, and anything else there is to pick up, such as
what's happening to our cows."

"Nosey cuss, ain't you?"

"Always have been," Don agreed. "Well, it was just a
thought. There's no reason you should get mixed up in it."

"You said it," the Kelso Kid nodded. "Anything else
you'd like to know?"

"Why yes, there is, now that you ask. I wouldn't object
to knowing something about that younger girl—which room
she sleeps in, whether she ever leaves the place alone, stuff
like that."

Red Marlowe gasped.

"You ain't planning to go over there, are you? Old Man
Culver'll have you killed sure as I'm a foot tall."

"If he does, I can't say he didn't warn me," Don grinned.
"However, before this is over, I'm going to have to talk
to that girl. Seems like that's the only way of finding out
who the baby's pa is."

"Maybe it is and maybe it ain't," the Kelso Kid said
slyly, and began to scratch.

"What're you driving at?"

The Kelso Kid grinned. "You could wait and ask the
baby, couldn't you?"

This made Red Marlowe bristle.

"I suppose that was intended to be funny or something. Anybody'd think what happened to Sammy was just a great big joke. Maybe if you'd known him like I did, or if . . ."

"Oh hell!" the Kelso Kid snorted disgustedly. "Now *he's* off again." He picked up his saddle and bridle and left the cabin.

Red Marlowe stared at the door so intently that Don had to speak to him twice before he heard. He turned to look at Don blankly.

"Did you say something?"

"I just said not to take it so hard. The Kelso Kid didn't intend that as a slap at Sammy."

Red didn't answer, so Don said sharply, "I'm leaving now. You'd better lock the door, and don't take any chances."

"All right," Red said, still acting a little bemused. However, he slid the bolt shut after Don left.

The Kelso Kid came into sight, leading his horse, and stopped in front of the cabin to throw the saddle across its back and tighten the cinch. He spat in the dirt, and said sourly, "You'd better get rid of that redhead, Harding. He's like a horse that ain't been properly broke. About the time you need him the worst, he'll start to buck."

"He's young. Likely he'll get over it."

"It's your funeral, mister." Kelso grinned. "Give my regards to the girls at Ruby Salmon's."

"I'll do that," Don promised.

He watched Kelso ride off toward the creek, then he went around to the corral and opened the gate. His sorrel butted against his shoulder as he led it into the yard, then it stood quietly while he picked up his saddle and settled it into place. Minutes later, Don mounted and took off toward town.

Less than two hours later, he came within sight of Paradise, and was surprised to find all the business places still lit up. It puzzled him until he started counting back and realized that this was a Saturday, when the ranchers and most of their crews would be in town.

In one way this was good, since there was a greater chance that whoever was spreading the lies about his encounter with Claire Culver would be more likely to be on hand. In another way it was bad. Saturday night was the time for blowing off steam, and men who had worked hard all week were liable to be a little excitable. However, he had dealt with cowpunchers most of his life, either as one of them or as a town marshal, and he thought he understood them pretty well. They were a tough, hard-nosed lot, but unless they were drunk, they believed in fair play. He checked the loads in his gun, mostly from habit, and rode boldly into the main street.

On this Saturday night, Paradise looked quite a bit different from the way he had last seen it. At least a score of cow ponies were tied at the various hitching rails, and three or four buggies stood parallel to one or the other of the wooden sidewalks.

Sound poured out of the saloon entrance, the low rumble of men's voices, the clink of glasses, and the occasional forced laughter of a woman. Don supposed that the big house with the red curtains would be doing a land-office business. Even as he dismounted in front of the cafe, a rather unsteady cowboy and a woman in a low-cut spangled dress came out of the saloon and disappeared into the darkness.

Someone in front of the saloon made a remark Don couldn't catch, and a second voice responded with an appreciative guffaw.

Don peered at the men from the shadow of his hat brim, and could see their dark shapes against the front of the saloon. He let his gaze move along to the sheriff's office, which was dark, and, still closer, to the cafe window. In spite of the late hour, there were several diners at the tables, including a woman with her back to the window. Don loosened the sorrel's cinch, crossed the sidewalk, and went in.

From this new vantage point, he was able to see that there were four customers in all, the woman whose back was toward the window, a round-faced little man facing her across the table, and two other men who looked like cowhands.

All four had turned to watch Don come in, as was to be expected in a town of this size, where any stranger was an item of interest. The two cowhands sized him up with only normal curiosity, their eyes paying particular attention to his tied-down holster. The brief inspection over, they returned their attention to their plates.

From the reaction of the round-faced man, Don surmised that he was one of those who had watched him that first day from behind some dim window. His face changed color, and he seemed to be trying to make himself even smaller. When the woman opposite him would have spoken, he shook his head.

Don took his eyes off the couple and moved to an unoccupied table. As he sat down, Helen Sprecher came out of the back room.

Either she had seen him come in, or she was hard to surprise, for she said matter-of-factly, "Good evening, Mr. Harding. What can I bring you?"

At mention of his name, both the cowhands looked around, their eyes suddenly alert. Don ignored them, and said, "I wouldn't refuse a piece of apple pie if there is any. I understand that's a specialty of yours."

She smiled, but accompanied the smile with a shake of her head.

"I'm sorry, but there isn't any apple pie tonight. There won't be any until Mr. Dowdall brings in some more apples. I can give you gooseberry if you like it."

"Gooseberry'll be fine, along with a cup of coffee."

She nodded and returned to the kitchen. Don glanced at the two men and saw that they were preparing to leave. A look at their plates twisted his lips in a wry grin. It wasn't often you saw a cowboy walk away leaving half his supper.

That was what they did, however, after laying some coins on the table. Before the door had swung shut behind them, the round-faced man and his wife—she was obviously that from the way she looked at him—hurried out after them. Don looked away from the front door and saw Helen Sprecher frowning in the kitchen doorway.

"What got into them?" she asked. "Did something happen?"

"Just me, miss. I have a queer effect on folks, especially the ones here in Paradise. They started getting itchy feet just as soon as you mentioned my name."

"Oh," she said. "I'm sorry. I didn't . . ."

"Nothing to worry about, miss. In fact it suits me fine,

so long as I haven't driven them away for good. I wanted a chance to talk to you alone, anyway."

"Well, it seems you have it," she added dryly, "Unless you count the ones looking in the window, that is."

"Let them look, so long as they can't hear what we say. First off, I want to thank you for the pie."

"You're welcome."

"And for the note," Don went on. "That's really what brought me to town tonight, that and a report from the Kelso Kid along the same lines."

"Just a minute," Helen said, and disappeared into the kitchen, returning presently with the pie and coffee. "As long as we have an audience, you'd better act like a customer. Now go on with what you were saying."

"All right, but understand, you can shut me up anytime you want to. I don't aim to get you mixed up in anything just because you were kind enough to warn me what was going on."

"Eat some pie," she said. "They're watching."

Don grinned, and took a bite of the pie.

"It's good. Not as good as the apple, but still mighty tasty. Now about those rumors. Would you have any idea who's spreading them?"

She was silent and stepped across to the other tables and gathered up the plates. When she had taken them to the kitchen, she came back with the coffee pot and refilled Don's cup.

"Maybe I shouldn't tell you this, Mr. Harding; it might just get you into even worse trouble. Nevertheless, I'm going to, mainly because I feel as you do, that your brother was hanged for a crime he didn't commit."

"Thank you," Don said, but she didn't seem to hear him.

"As you know, this building is next door to the sheriff's office. When my back window and his back door are both open, I sometimes overhear what's being said over there, although I occasionally wish I couldn't." She leaned down as though to straighten his cup on the saucer, and added in a lower tone, "Two days ago, the sheriff had a visitor, and I heard part of the conversation. Enough to know that it was one of the crew from Mr. Culver's Box C. I heard the name, 'Miss Culver.'"

"Miss Claire Culver, I bet," Don said, his eyes suddenly hard. "That's all I need to know, miss. I'm obliged to you." He rose to his feet.

"What do you plan to do?" she asked worriedly. "You don't intend to face the sheriff with this tonight? with the town crowded?"

"Why not? It was a crowd that lynched Sammy, wasn't it?" He grinned and pointed at his plate. "Seems like I'm getting as bad as the rest of your customers. I'm leaving half my supper."

CHAPTER TWELVE

As HELEN HAD remarked, there were several onlookers clustered around the front of the cafe, including the two men who had left their suppers unfinished to spread the word. Don let the door swing shut behind him, then paused to roll himself a cigarette. He went about it deliberately, meanwhile gauging the temper of the crowd with his eyes.

Most of them looked like cowhands enjoying a night in town. Their expressions indicated curiosity more than anything else. So far, at least, they were neutral, although no one knew better than Don how quickly this could change. He was also aware of the fact that few if any of these men had participated in the lynching, which had been carried out by townsmen.

His cigarette lit, Don singled out one of the group, a beefy individual who looked as though he might have some authority, and said evenly, "I see Sheriff Yankton isn't in his office. Would you have any idea where I'd be likely to find him?"

After a brief hesitation, the man said, "Chances are you

won't. They tell me he's been out of town since noon. I don't know when he expects to be back."

"Thanks."

Hiding his disappointment, Don crossed the walk toward the hitchrail, the men moving apart to let him through. It had not occurred to him that the sheriff might be away. Since this was a Saturday night, Yankton's absence seemed all the more unusual. In most towns, a lawman really earned his pay on Saturday. However, if he wasn't here, he wasn't here. It came as an anti-climax, but all Don could do now was wait for him to return, and, while he was waiting, the sorrel could just as well be comfortable. He undid the reins, and, rather than tighten the cinch, led the horse across to the livery stable.

Will Tully was sitting outside the entrance on a bale of hay; yellow light was shining on his bare head from a lantern suspended over the doorway. He got up to follow Don in, and said courteously, "Nice evening, Mr. Harding. Are you staying in town all night?"

"That depends on a number of things," Don said. "One of them being how soon the sheriff gets back. At any rate, I'll be here long enough to use one of your stalls."

"Help yourself to any that's empty," Tully said. "Or I'll take care of him myself if you want me to."

"Never mind. I'm in no hurry now." Don led the sorrel into a clean stall, and changed the bridle for a halter which was tied there for that purpose. He removed the saddle and left the stall to lay it on a rack; then he came back and began rubbing the horse with a piece of burlap he had picked up.

Will Tully watched him in silence a few minutes, then said curiously, "You were saying it depended on a number of things. Any of them things I'd know about?"

"Probably," Don said, and looked at him across the sorrel's rump. "The trouble is, you're not likely to want to talk about them. For instance, who started the rumor about me and Claire Culver?"

Tully didn't answer, and Don said quietly, "See what I mean? Folks here in Paradise will talk about anything, so long as it's the weather. Instead of Paradise, the place should be called Cowardice."

"Now hold on a minute," Tully objected, flushing. "You've got no call saying things like that. Not to me, anyhow. I had no part in lynching your brother."

"No? What you probably mean is that you didn't actually put the rope around his neck. Well, maybe you're right, but that doesn't mean you're not as guilty as the others. Tell me something; did you raise even one finger to stop it?"

Tully couldn't meet Don's eyes, and Don went on bluntly, "That's what I figured. You crawled into your shell till it was over, so now you think you're better than the ones in the mob."

"Well, damn it," Tully protested. "What else could I do? Time I found out about it, nobody could've stopped 'em." He glared at Don accusingly. "What do you think I should've done? got myself killed? Maybe you've never seen a mob after it got started."

"I've seen three of them in my life," Don said. "And I don't want to see a fourth, especially not from the end of a rope. But I don't see any mob out in the street right now, so you can't use that for an excuse."

The temperature in the barn wasn't warm enough to make anyone sweat, but Tully had to mop beads of perspiration from his forehead. Finally he groaned, and said defeatedly, "All right. I heard it from Seth Huddleson. There's no use trying to make me tell you any more, because that's all there is. Now will you let me alone?"

"I'll be glad to," Don said. "Take good care of my horse."

Tully didn't answer, so Don left the barn and headed for the hotel. This might be a roundabout way of getting at the truth, but with the sheriff missing, it was the best he could think of.

The hotelman was behind his desk, struggling over some ledgers. He looked up with annoyance which changed quickly to surprise, then to alarm, as he recognized his visitor. For once, he apparently had forgotten to keep abreast of what was going on in town.

Don crossed the lobby to the desk, and Huddleson backed up against the wall, his eyes wide with terror. He licked his lips, and said hoarsely, "Now hold on, Mr. Harding. You've got no right to . . ." He stuttered to a stop.

"No right to what?" Don asked. "To come into a hotel and ask a question? Aren't you open to the public anymore?"

"Y-yes sir," Huddleson stammered. "But you look like . . ." He swallowed painfully. "*What* question, Mr. Harding?"

Don looked at him across the desk, and smiled.

"It could be about a lot of things, I suppose. For instance I could ask you if you ever found that rattlesnake you had someone throw onto my bed. I've been wondering about that. A snake isn't easy to find when it's had its rattles cut off."

Huddleson threw a frantic look toward the street, found no help there and focused his bulging eyes on Don.

"I don't know what you're talking about, Mr. Harding. All that about rattlesnakes. I didn't . . ."

"Then it's a good thing that isn't my question," Don said mildly. "I just brought it up to remind you what can happen to a man when he makes a mistake. What I wanted to ask you now is entirely different, but a wrong answer could get you into just as much trouble. Who is it that's spreading the lies about me and Claire Culver?"

Huddleson was trembling so badly that when he shook his head the movement was hardly noticeable. He made two or three false starts, then managed to say, "I haven't heard anything about . . ."

Don reached across the counter and grabbed the front of Huddleson's vest.

"You can talk plainer than that, Huddleson. Try again."

The hotelman clawed ineffectively at Don's hand. Suddenly the starch went out of him, and he said in a whisper, "Charlie Clute told it to me. That's all I know about it, so help me."

"Charlie Clute?"

"The pill roller," Huddleson whimpered, and pointed vaguely in the direction of the pharmacy.

"I'm obliged to you," Don said, and let go of Huddleson's vest. He crossed the lobby, but turned short of the door. "About that snake—I turned it loose that same night. Outdoors."

Huddleson was too exhausted for the information to have any effect.

~ This time, when Don stepped onto the sidewalk, he saw a little knot of men watching him from in front of the unlighted sheriff's office. They kept even with him as he passed the bank and the vacant lot and came to the pharmacy. When he went inside, they stopped to watch him from in front of the general store.

The woman he had seen in the cafe was behind the counter. She regarded him with more than casual interest, and said nervously, "We're closed for the night, mister; you'll have to come back tomorrow."

Don touched his hat brim respectfully, and said, "The door's still open, Mrs. Clute. Since I'm already in, I might as well do what I came for. Will you get your husband, please?"

"He isn't here."

"Then I reckon I'll just have to wait." He walked slowly toward a door near the back of the store, pretending to be interested in some patent medicine advertisements on the wall. When he came to the door, he reached out suddenly and jerked it open. The round-faced man he had seen in the cafe almost fell into the room.

"Looks like I'm in luck," Don said. "You're the man I was waiting for, and here you are." He took Clute's arm and drew him away from the door, then closed it behind him so he couldn't duck out.

"We're shut down for the night," Clute said desperately.

"So your wife just told me, but I won't take much of your time. Not unless you turn stubborn, in which case I may as well tell you right now that I've already talked to two of the town's leading citizens, and persuaded them to talk, so you'll save us both a lot of trouble if you speak right up. Who was it that told you the lie about Claire Culver and me?"

Clute shot a quick glance at his wife, let out his breath in a quavering sigh, and said dully, "I knew this was bound to come, soon as Niles Dowdall told it to me. Damn it, why didn't he . . ."

"Thank you," Don said. He nodded to the woman, and left the pharmacy.

The group of men had been augmented by two or three

newcomers, and they occupied most of the sidewalk in front of the general store. Don crossed directly toward them, but he was forced to stop short when one of them refused to move out of the way. He was a lanky, red-faced man with a crooked nose, and he stared at Don belligerently.

Don would have gone around him, but the man side-stepped so as to continue to block his passage.

"Going someplace, mister?" he asked sarcastically.

Don's patience was already worn pretty thin, so he was in no mood to stand and argue. However, there was no hint of anger in his own voice when he spoke.

"Why, yes, stranger. As a matter of fact, I'm going into this store."

"That's what you think," the man growled, and swung a haymaker which was intended to take Don's head off his shoulders.

Instead, Don ducked beneath it, and drove a right into the man's midsection, following it with a jolting left and another right. The stranger grunted with surprise and pain, and dropped his arms across his belly, whereupon Don reached up, hooked a hand behind the fellow's neck, and slammed him downward onto the road.

Someone in the group whistled softly, and another said, "Mister, do you know who that is you just knocked hell out of?"

"No," Don said. "But he probably doesn't know who I am, so we're even." He stepped onto the walk, where a wide path opened as though by magic, and kicked open the door of the mercantile.

Niles Dowdall had been watching him through the door, and had to jump out of the way. Before Don could speak, Dowdall held out his hands and said pleadingly, "Don't start anything in here, mister. I saw what you did to that feller out front. Just tell me what you want me to do, and I'll do it."

"All right, Dowdall. Who was it that passed you the word I tried to step out of line with the Culver girl?"

Dowdall glanced toward the street, and edged away from the door; Don followed him. When they were as far from the door as possible, the merchant said thinly, "It

was Sheriff Yankton, mister, but for God's sake don't tell
him I said so."

"Maybe I won't," Don said, "provided you'll go across
the street and tell Clute the whole thing was a lie."

"Yes, sir. I'll do that."

"Good. And tell Clute to pass the word along to the
others. In an hour or so, I'll check with the last man on
the line. If word hasn't reached him by then, I'll start
working back." He turned and left the store.

The man he had hit was being helped across toward
the pharmacy by two of the others, so apparently he needed
patching up, probably where he had lit on his face. The
rest of the onlookers had disappeared, presumably having
returned to the saloon to talk about what they had just wit-
nessed.

Now that it was over, Don's nerves were a little jumpy.
It was always that way with him; as long as there was
some physical outlet for his anger, he remained perfectly
calm, but when the emergency was over, reaction set in.
While he waited for the feeling to pass, he made a cigarette
and lit it. By the time the cigarette was smoked, his nerves
were steady again. It came to him that he had gone a long
way around to get back almost to where he had started.
Helen Sprecher's information had practically convinced
him that the sheriff was primarily responsible for circulating
the rumor; now there was no question about it.

He moved away from the front of the store, and went as
far as the sheriff's office to make sure Yankton hadn't returned, noting as he did that the cafe was now dark. Since
it seemed likely that the sheriff would be getting back before long, he decided to go to the saloon and wait.

The Dancing Lady was running full blast. At least half
a dozen men were bellied up to the bar, and four or five
others were making awkward attempts at dancing with an
equal number of women, or were just hanging on and making
no pretense of dancing.

Don crossed to the bar, found an empty spot near one
end, and signaled the bartender, who promptly set a bottle
of whiskey in front of him, and put a glass beside it.

From the way Don was being looked at, it was obvious

that everyone in the place had heard about his encounter with the broken-nosed stranger. Don tried to ignore their stares, but he couldn't help being aware of the attention he was getting. After a bit, one of the women left the man she was with and moved up beside him at the bar. She was somewhat older than the others, but still retained some semblance of what must have once been real beauty.

"You look lonesome, mister. Want to buy a girl a drink?"

"I'll be glad to." Don motioned to the bartender for another glass, and filled it from the bottle. The woman downed it without stopping for breath.

"Thanks, mister. I suppose there's nothing else I . . ."

Don shook his head, and said, "I'm waiting for the sheriff." He would have refilled her glass, but she put her hand over it.

"That's plenty, thanks. I wasn't really thirsty, just curious. They're all talking about you."

"They?"

"Everybody." She nodded toward the room in general. "These boys out here, and the card players in the back room. It isn't often that they see a man like Coley Lamson knocked cold."

"Just luck," Don said. "He probably wasn't expecting it."

"Probably not. You strike me as a man who does unexpected things." She smiled. "Well, I already know your name, Don Harding. In case you don't know mine, I'm Ruby Samson. I have a house here in town. Sort of a finishing school for females."

"I've heard of it," Don said solemnly. "In fact, I believe I've noticed your pennant. It's unusual, to say the least."

"You should've seen the girl they belonged to," she remarked. "Well, drop around anytime."

"Thanks. Oh, by the way, the Kelso Kid sent his regards."

She laughed, and started back to one of the tables. Don was smiling at her back, when a rough voice said bluntly, "All right, Harding, put up your hands. You're under arrest."

Surprised, and angry with himself for being caught off guard, Don turned slowly toward the source of the command. He saw Sheriff Yankton just inside the door of the card-

room, a double-barrelled shotgun pointed at Don's belly.
Yankton's ugly face was twisted in a triumphant sneer.

"Just you make one move," he warned, "and I'll blow
your guts out."

"I bet it wouldn't be the first time," Don said. "The first
time you got the drop on a man and killed him without
giving him a chance, I mean. Is that how you got your
reputation?"

"Shut up!" Yankton snarled. "Or by God, I'll let you
have it."

"Don't you intend to anyway?" Don demanded, too angry
to be cautious. "By the way, you forgot to mention what
you're arresting me for. If it has anything to do with that
deal the Culver girl and you rigged up, you're wasting your
time. Before you could get away with that, Whitey Larson
would tell what really happened."

The sheriff looked startled at Don's mention of Claire
Culver, but he recovered quickly.

"That ain't it at all, Harding, although I intend to look
into that, too. What I'm arresting you for is something else.
Maybe it's different wherever you come from, but out here,
when a man beats up a deputy sheriff going about his job,
we don't just laugh it off."

"A deputy sheriff? What kind of trick are you trying to
pull now?"

"No trick, mister. My deputy, Coley Lamson, tried to
ask you a civil question, and you hauled off and hit him.
Hell, there's no use denying it. I've got a dozen witnesses."
Without taking his eyes off Don, he yelled, "Come on in,
Coley. Let everyone see for themselves."

The broken-nosed man came out of the back room, his
face scarred where he had skidded in the road. He glowered
at Don, and pointed a dirty finger.

"That's the man, Sheriff. That's the son-of-a-bitch that
hit me."

Don wasn't interested in the accusation. What had at-
tracted his attention was the shiny star pinned to the man's
shirt. A star which he was sure hadn't been there an hour
earlier.

CHAPTER THIRTEEN

For a moment after Coley Lamson finished talking, the saloon was perfectly silent. During that moment, Don made up his mind not to submit to being put in jail. The charge on which Yankton was arresting him was of no consequence in itself. In fact, if it came to an actual trial, with witnesses sworn to tell the truth, there would be no problem of proving that Lamson had provoked the fight himself and that he had worn no deputy's badge at the time, if indeed he had *ever* worn one.

What made Don determine to stay out of jail was the very trumped-up nature of the charge. If Yankton—or someone whose orders Yankton took—wanted him out of circulation for a few days, there must be a better reason than the one on the surface. And Don couldn't forget that Red Marlowe was alone at H Bar H.

Sheriff Yankton took a step away from the card room, and said savagely, "All right, Harding, you heard what I said. I'm putting you in jail. Unbuckle your gunbelt and let it drop."

"Suppose *you* unbuckle it," Don said mildly. "After what you told me about blowing my guts out if I made a move, I'm not foolish enough to lower my hands."

"By God you'd better, or I'll fill you full of buckshot!"

"In front of all these voters?" Don shook his head. "You're a yellow bastard, Yankton, but you aren't going to pull a stunt like that. What would folks say about a lawman who murdered a prisoner in cold blood? What would your boss, Cletus Culver, say?"

For a second, Don was afraid he had gone too far. It was his intention to goad Yankton into doing something

105

reckless; judging from Yankton's expression now, it was beginning to look as though that reckless act might be the
firing of the shotgun.

With a visible effort, Yankton got control of himself.

"Go ahead, Harding. Play it cute, and see how far it gets
you. Coley, go over there and take his gun."

Don shifted his gaze to Lamson. If the man were actually
a real deputy, the jig was up. Don was staking everything
on his belief that the tin star had been his for less than an
hour.

His hunch received support when Lamson drew a pistol,
aimed it at Don's head, and came straight toward him;
apparently he was oblivious to the fact that this would put
him directly between Don and the sheriff's shotgun. Don
knew that a real lawman would have had sense enough
to circle and approach from the side.

At this, Don pretended to give in. He said dejectedly,
"All right, Sheriff, you win. I'll shuck my gun. First, though,
I have to untie this string around my leg." Without allowing
Lamson's sluggish mind time to analyze this, he bent down
and fumbled with the buckskin thong. Suddenly, in one
fluid motion which was the result of years of practice, he
straightened up with his pistol in his hand. It spurted flame,
and Lamson whirled as a bullet slammed into his right arm,
jarring the gun loose.

In a continuation of the same movement, Don charged
into Lamson's unbalanced body, slamming him into the
sheriff. Before Yankton could untangle himself, Don's pistol
crashed down on top of his skull. The sheriff's eyes went
blank, and he crumpled to the floor.

Don kicked Lamson's dropped pistol into a corner and
sent the shotgun skidding after it. He spun around the end
of the bar, put his back to the mirror, and faced the room.

"Just like you are, all of you, and no one gets hurt. I
didn't plan it this way, but it couldn't be helped. You all
know that this man—" he pointed at Lamson, who was staring stupidly at the spreading red stain on his right sleeve—
"—that this man wasn't a deputy until Yankton figured
it would be a good way of getting me thrown in jail. I'm in
favor of law and order, but I don't intend to sit still while

someone hangs a frame around my neck." He holstered his pistol and moved out from behind the bar.

"Now I'm going to get my horse and ride out. If anybody wants to try and stop me, this is the time."

Nobody moved. He crossed the barroom and stepped onto the sidewalk, his breath sighing out with relief when the batwings swung together behind him.

Nothing on the street had changed, except that one of the buggies had pulled out, and the sheriff's horse was now in front of his office, where a lamp glowed inside the room. Apparently, Yankton had returned to town, learned what had happened between Don and Lamson, and cooked up this scheme to place him under arrest. No doubt, he had left his office by the rear door and had come into the saloon through the card room. It wasn't his method, however, which worried Don, but his reason. If Yankton had been out at Box C, receiving instructions from Cletus Culver, this attempted arrest could indicate that Culver had decided to carry out his threat to run Don out of the country.

There was one favorable factor. Culver could not have anticipated that Don would be in town, or that the sheriff would so promptly find an excuse for arresting him. There might still be time to get to the ranch before Culver made his move. Walking rapidly, Don crossed to the livery stable and went in.

Will Tully was still up, probably waiting for some of his customers to come and claim their horses. He looked up uneasily, but didn't speak until Don had finished saddling the sorrel and was about to back it out of the stall. Then he said in a low voice, "They tell me you beat hell out of Coley Lamson. It's something he's needed for a long time, but there's one thing you ought to know; Lamson and the sheriff are thick as thieves. When the sheriff finds out about it, you're going to be in trouble."

"He already has, and I already am," Don said. He backed the sorrel into the aisle, and gave Tully a searching look. "Tell me something, Tully; how come you bothered to warn me about this? Didn't you say you weren't going to give me any more information?"

"A man can change his mind, can't he?" Tully grumbled, and added quickly, "Now don't get me wrong, Mr. Harding. I ain't dealing myself in on your private war; it's just that—well, maybe I can't help admiring a man that don't know when he's licked."

"I'll settle for that," Don said. "However, I'm not licked. Not yet, anyway." He pulled himself into the saddle, and turned for a last word. "If you don't think it'll be sticking your neck out, how about looking the other way while I ride out? Then you can honestly tell them you didn't see me leave?"

Tully rubbed his chin, then crossed to the back of the barn and disappeared into his living quarters.

As he did, Don heard the clomp of hoofs out in the street. He reined up just inside the entrance, and leaned over to squint around the edge of the doorway.

What he saw made him swear under his breath. Whitey Larson and three other riders were pulling up in front of the Dancing Lady, where lamplight spilled over the swinging doors. As they got out of their saddles, the saloon doors swung open, and Sheriff Yankton came into sight, holding onto the doorframe for support. There was a moment's stunned silence, then two of the three men began asking questions at the same time. A dark shadow detached itself from the front of the cafe to join them, and an arm pointed toward the livery stable.

"He's over at Will Tully's," a voice said thickly. "I seen him go in, and he ain't come out yet."

There was no point making a run for it now, not with upwards of a dozen men looking at the door of the livery stable. Don swung down from the saddle, ran to the back of the room, and burst into Tully's living quarters.

"Someone saw me come in here, and they're on their way across the street right now, so I'm going to use your back door. If they get rough about it, tell them I held a gun on you."

"They'll never believe it," Tully said glumly. "Some of 'em are sore at me already for making that grave marker. You'd better knock me out." He stuck out his chin.

"Good Lord! I can't . . ."

"Go on!" Tully pleaded. "It's the only way to convince 'em."

Already there were men's voices in the barn. Don gritted

his teeth and smashed a fist into Tully's jaw. The liveryman dropped like a poleaxed steer. Don stepped across him and let himself out through the back door.

There were no lights visible here, but the starlight was sufficient to make objects recognizable. It would also reveal Don's presence as soon as someone came looking. He turned east, away from the main part of town, and walked as rapidly as he could without risking tripping over the trash which littered the area. Before he had gone a hundred yards, men's voices reached him from the spot he had just left.

"Spread out!" Sheriff Yankton growled. "He can't have gone far. Larson, you and your men take the other side of the street, in case he manages to get across before we catch him."

Don cursed silently, for it was exactly what he was planning to do, since there was obviously no hiding place on this side of the street. Now he knew he had to move fast, before Whitey Larson and the Box C men reached the road. He bent low and ran across the street, gambling that everyone's attention would be centered on the livery stable.

The gamble paid off; at least no one raised an alarm. Don circled to the back of the saddle shop, darted across the vacant lot next door, and flattened himself against the rear end of the cafe.

The maneuver had bought him a few seconds' grace, but that was all. Unless he could find a safer spot than this, he was sure to be discovered. He considered tapping on Helen Sprecher's window. In fact, he even raised his knuckles toward the glass before deciding against it. If it came to a house to house search, he didn't want her implicated.

Shouts came to him from the street, the sound increasing in volume. He looked around desperately, saw Ruby Salmon's big house, with lamplight showing dimly through the red curtains, and grinned. Ruby had invited him to come see her anytime—why not now? No doubt he wouldn't be the first man who had approached the place furtively under cover of darkness. He left the back of the cafe and headed in that direction.

The Palace of Venus, if not the most respectable establishment in town, was certainly the most ornate. This was not due to any desire on Ruby Salmon's part to be ostentatious.

In fact, if she had believed that it would be better business to operate in a tent, she would have done so, for she was first of all a good businesswoman, and she considered the Palace as much a commercial enterprise as the hotel or the saloon. Her chief reason for insisting on the thickest carpets and most expensive furniture was the effect they had on the behavior of her customers. Even dusty and lusty trailhands were a little overawed by such surroundings, and hesitated to indulge in the rough horseplay which would have seemed natural in an ordinary crib.

Among other luxuries, Ruby's place had a roofed porch across the front, where customers could wait comfortably out of sight until they were admitted. Don stepped onto this porch now, grateful for the shelter it provided, and twisted a brass knob which rang a bell on the inside of the door.

After what seemed a long time, during which Don heard the men's voices grow louder and saw shadows against the backs of the buildings along this side of the street, the door opened a crack, and a woman's voice said politely, "Just have a seat on the porch, mister. You'll be called."

The door started to close, but Don put his hand against it. "Are you Ruby Salmon, ma'am? I'd like to talk to you."

"Who are you?"

"Don Harding. I was talking to you over at the saloon a few minutes ago."

"Just a minute." She closed the door, a chain rattled, and the door opened wide. "Come in, Mr. Harding. I hardly expected to see you here tonight, but as I may have mentioned, you strike me as a man who does unexpected things." She smiled. "For instance, like going up against a pistol and a shotgun, and getting away with it."

Don had stepped quickly through the opening, and closed the door behind him. He grinned, and said, "I can thank Coley Lamson's clumsiness for that. This makes twice I've been lucky where he's concerned. However, it seems my luck's run out. Whitey Larson and some of his crew got to town before I could leave. They're taking the place to pieces looking for me, along with the sheriff and a dozen others."

"Then *that's* why you're here, not because you couldn't resist my charms." Ruby sighed in mock chagrin. "I've heard all kinds of reasons, but never this one. I suppose what I *should* do is open the door and start screaming."

"No question about it," Don said. "That's your civic duty."

"Civic duty be damned, Mr. Harding. If it was up to the citizens of Paradise, the majority would ship me out of town on the next stagecoach."

"Then why haven't they?"

"Why?" She smiled knowingly. "Because they're afraid to, that's why. If I wanted to, I could tell things about some of our sanctimonious merchants that would make your hair curl. It's amazing what men will talk about when they're..." She coughed. "When they're under an emotional strain."

On impulse, Don said, "I don't suppose what they've said throws any light on what really happened to Minnie Culver."

"That's the one thing they don't talk about. In fact it's probably what some of them come here to forget." Her lips curved into an odd smile. "If it so happens that your brother was innocent, there's liable to be some man leaving town in a hurry three or four months from now. I can't wait to see who it'll be."

Don recalled what the Kelso Kid had said about waiting to ask the baby who its father was. Now that he coupled this with Ruby Salmon's remark, it began to make sense. If Minnie's baby should look like its father...

A step on the porch interrupted his thoughts, and he whirled to face the door, his hand dropping to his pistol. Then Ruby Salmon put a finger to her lips, and pointed at a curtained doorway. Don pushed aside the curtain and saw that it covered a small closet in which several garments were hanging. He stepped inside, and let the curtain drop back into place just as the bell jangled violently.

Through the crack at the edge of the curtain, Don watched Ruby hook the chain and open the door a few inches. "Who is it?"

"It's me, Ruby," the sheriff's voice said irritably. "Open up. I'm looking for a man."

"A man?" Ruby laughed. "Aren't you a little mixed up, Sheriff?"

"Damn it, you know that ain't what I meant. You saw

that bastard of a Harding hit me on the head. He got away, and we're looking for him. Let me in."

"Of course, Sheriff." She closed the door far enough so that she could unhook the chain, then pulled it all the way open. "Come right in."

The sheriff came through the doorway, eyes wary and six-shooter in hand. He let his gaze rest a moment on the closet, and Don noiselessly lifted the gun out of his holster.

"What's behind the curtain?" Yankton demanded.

"You might find almost anything," Ruby said carelessly. "Anything except the man you're looking for, that is. If Harding's the bastard you claim he is, and if he was in that closet, by now you'd probably be bleeding all over my good rug." She waved a hand toward the closet. "Go ahead and look if you want to. Maybe one of those hats in there is yours."

Yankton stared at the curtain a moment longer, looking a little foolish, then muttered something under his breath and holstered his gun. "All right, if you say he ain't there, I'll take your word for it."

"You'll do nothing of the sort," Ruby said. "I haven't said he isn't there. Since it was you who let him get away, finding him is *your* responsibility, not mine. If you want to search the house, go ahead and do it, but don't blame me for anything that happens. Some of my customers are a little touchy. If you *aren't* going to, get out and let me close the door."

"Damn you, Ruby, you're too independent."

"Maybe it's because I'm used to being my own boss, Sheriff."

"What's that supposed to mean?"

"Anything you want it to. By the way, how's everything out at the Culver place?"

The sheriff's jaw shot out, and for a moment Don thought he would do something rash. Then he whirled on his heel, jerked the door open, and stalked out of the room. Ruby stood in the open doorway watching, then closed the door and slid the bolt.

"Whew!" Don said, stepping out of the closet. "You sure treated him rough. He came within an inch of hitting you. What was the idea?"

"I wanted to make him mad enough so he'd forget what he came in for. Right now he's so sore at me he can't think of anything else. In about ten minutes, he'll begin to realize you really might have been in that closet. Then he'll be back."

"In that case, I'd better not be here." Don moved toward the door.

"Wait. You can't go out that way. There's a back door they may not be watching. There're also three or four saddled horses tied out back. Help yourself."

"What happens when the owner wants to use it?"

"I'll let him think you borrowed it on your own. He doesn't need to know I had anything to do with it. Now you'd better go, while there's still a chance."

"I'm leaving," Don said. "But first, how come you're going to so much trouble for someone you never even saw until an hour ago?"

"Oh, I saw you before that. In fact, I was watching from my upstairs window when you went looking for your brother's grave. And I also drove close enough to see the board you put over it. I never knew Sammy, but the way it looks to me, anyone whose brother thinks as much of him as you do of Sammy can't be so bad. And anyone who..." She shook her head. "This is getting all tangled up, and besides, it had nothing to do with my giving you a break."

"Then what did, ma'am?"

"Well, let's say it's because you bought me a drink tonight without acting as if it was a down payment. Now get going."

"I'm gone," Don said. "I'm obliged to you for everything."

"You needn't be. I've been waiting a long time to tell off the sheriff." She smiled. "Say hello to that old buzzard of a Kelso Kid."

"I will." Don stepped aside to let her pass, then followed her to the back door. Soon thereafter, he rode out on a borrowed horse. As he looked back, it occurred to him that three of Paradise's citizens had now done him good turns: Helen Sprecher, Ruby Salmon, and Will Tully. Was it possible that he was being too harsh in his judgment of the town?

CHAPTER FOURTEEN

THE HORSE WHICH Don Harding rode away from Ruby Salmon's back door was not the only one to be used that night without its owner's knowledge or consent. By the time Don reached the turn off to H Bar H, another purloined mount was being ridden out of town toward the west. Its rider was Helen Sprecher.

When Helen had closed the cafe for the night, she had fully intended to follow her usual nightly routine of bathing, brushing her hair, perhaps reading for an hour or so, and then going to sleep. Well, at least to bed; so much had happened in the last few hours that she couldn't be sure of going to sleep immediately.

That had been her intention. However, before reaching the door to her bedroom, she had heard the sounds of an approaching rider in the street, followed by the creak of saddle leather. Retracing her steps across the darkened cafe, she had reached the front window in time to see Sheriff Yankton tying his horse at the rail.

This had worried her, for she was aware of the fight between Don Harding and Coley Lamson, and she also knew that Lamson and the sheriff were cronies, a circumstance which was attested to when Lamson appeared out of the darkness and joined Yankton at the office door. Due to the angle of the window, Helen could not see the doorway itself, but the sound of footsteps next door indicated that both men had gone inside.

The thin wooden partition that separated the cafe from the sheriff's office was usually no bar to hearing the conversations that went on in there. Tonight, however, after one brief outburst from Coley Lamson, the voices became guarded. This increased Helen's uneasiness. But although

she unabashedly placed an ear against the wall, she couldn't
make out the words. She gave it up, and was halfway to
the bedroom door before it occurred to her that this was the
first time she had ever deliberately tried to eavesdrop.

Instead of lighting her bedroom lamp, she felt
her way across the familiar room and stood beside the window. After a bit, two men came out the back door of the
sheriff's office and entered the rear of the saloon. As they
were outlined momentarily in the light from the card room,
Helen recognized Lamson and the sheriff. She also noticed
that Yankton was carrying a shotgun.

She immediately connected their actions with Don Harding, who, she had been told, was in the saloon. Obviously,
their intentions were not peaceful, or Yankton wouldn't
have needed the shotgun. Somehow, she told herself, Don
should be warned.

But how? Even assuming that there would be time to
reach the saloon ahead of Yankton, what could she say?
The mere fact that the sheriff was carrying a shotgun didn't
prove that he intended to shoot anyone, certainly not that
he had designs against Don Harding. Rushing into the saloon now would only make both her and Don look foolish.
Besides, she had an idea that a man such as Don would
prefer to fight his own battles, without the help of a woman.
All she could do was wait and pray, as women had always
done when the men they loved . . .

Startled by the trend of her own thinking, Helen uttered
a dismayed gasp. What was the matter with her lately? She
and Don Harding weren't . . .

The sound of a shot brought her back to the present. She
stiffened, and waited breathlessly for it to be repeated.
When the seconds passed and it wasn't, she resumed her
breathing. Whatever had happened, at least nobody had
felt the blast of that shotgun. Even she could distinguish
between the sound of a shotgun and that of a pistol.

No one came out the back of the saloon, so she returned
to the front of the cafe on the chance that something might
be happening out in the street. She had just reached the
window when Don Harding came out of the saloon and
hurried across toward the livery stable.

From the sudden relief which almost made her dizzy, she

knew that there was no use fooling herself. Absurd though
it might be, she had fallen in love with a man she hardly
knew. A man-who probably thought of her—if he thought
of her at all—merely as the proprietress of a restaurant
where he had eaten a couple of times.

She watched Don enter the livery stable, then swung her
gaze toward the saloon, half expecting him to be followed.
Instead, the sidewalk remained empty, except for a man
in front of the cafe who didn't appear interested in what
was going on. She supposed he might be drunk.

For several minutes, the street was peaceful. Then everything happened at once. Four riders came into town from
the west; men poured out of the saloon; the idler in front
of the cafe suddenly came to life; and the street filled with
shouting men converging on the livery stable.

Helen waited tautly for gunshots, but they didn't come.
She unlocked the cafe door and opened it an inch so as to
hear better. When it became evident from the shouts that
Don had gotten away, she closed the door, leaned against
it a moment in the weakness of relief, then returned to the
bedroom. She was standing there by the window when Don
paused for a moment, raised his hand as though to rap,
then changed his mind and took off in the direction of Ruby
Salmon's. Moments later, a rectangle of light showed as
Ruby's door was opened.

Helen's heart was pounding so furiously that she backed
away from the window and sagged down on the edge of the
bed. When it had seemed that Don might rap on the glass,
she had known that she would open the window, regardless
of the consequences. In a way, she was glad that he hadn't,
since it would have been almost impossible to conceal a man
so close to the sheriff's office. In another, utterly illogical
way, she was distressed that he had chosen to turn to someone other than herself for help.

It came to her that she was being unbelievably foolish
about this. Not only that, but while she sat here acting like
a jealous schoolgirl, Don was still in grave danger. Even
if he should succeed in leaving town, he would only delay
the inevitable. So long as the townsmen resented his presence, so long as Sheriff Yankton was determined to get rid
of him, so long as Cletus Culver ...

It all came back to Mr. Culver. That was where the sheriff got his instructions; in fact, the whole town, with perhaps three exceptions: herself, Will Tully, and Ruby Salmon, was under Culver's thumb. And Culver hated Don Harding, not for anything he had done, but because his brother was supposed to have been responsible for what had happened to Minnie.

There were other men out back now, prowling about and shouting angrily. Helen returned to the window in time to see one of them cross over to Ruby Salmon's. The door opened, and she recognized the silhouette of Sheriff Yankton. Presently he went in, and the door was closed.

It was at this moment that Helen knew what she had to do. Let the men try to settle this in the only way they understood, with guns. All they would prove was who had the fastest draw and the steadiest nerves. What really mattered was the truth about what had happened to Minnie Culver. And this was something a woman might have a better chance than a man of finding out.

Without waiting for the sheriff to come out of Ruby Salmon's, Helen drew the curtains, lit a lamp, and changed into an old pair of Levi's and a man's shirt, the costume she usually wore for scrubbing out the cafe. She doused the light, let herself out the front door, and looked across at the livery stable.

Two men were in the stable entrance, apparently left on guard in case Don should try to come back for his horse. Their presence made it impossible for Helen to get one of Tully's horses without exciting curiosity. She considered the other possibilities a moment, made up her mind, and started along the sidewalk toward the west end of town; she counted on the darkness and her men's clothing to mask her identity.

At the far end of the block, two ponies were tied in front of the general store. Helen chose one at random, untied the reins, and boosted herself into the saddle. She wasn't an expert rider, and the horse seemed to sense the fact, but she got it turned in the right direction and it behaved well enough. Half an hour later, when she was well out of town, she lifted it into a canter.

Don was midway between the road and H Bar H when he heard the tattoo of hoofs. He reined up and swung his borrowed mount to face toward town, thinking the sound might indicate pursuit. However, it soon began to fade, so he assumed it was made by some cowhand heading back home. He turned his mount toward the ranch again, and touched spurs to its flanks.

He had gone perhaps a mile when he smelled wood smoke, faintly at first, as though it might be from a cookstove, then getting stronger as he rode. There was another odor with it, one which made his horse lift its head and snort; the rancid smell of burned flesh.

Don put spurs to his mount, keeping it at a run even though the route lay uphill. It was something he would never have done under normal conditions, but all he could think of now was that Red Marlowe was at the cabin, and that the smoke seemed to be in that direction.

The horse, its sides heaving, reached the ridge. Don took one agonized look into the valley, and pulled his faltering mount to a walk. No reason now to punish the animal. If anyone had been in that cabin, he was beyond human help. The roof had already fallen in, and was blazing fiercely within what was left of the four burning walls. As Don watched, the front wall fell outward in a shower of sparks.

The smell of burned flesh was so strong now that Don had to fight his horse to make it enter the clearing. He couldn't risk tying it for fear it would panic and snap the reins, so he stayed in the saddle and circled the clearing at its outer rim. Even here the heat was intense. However, he managed to get a look at the corral, and to see the blackened carcass of a horse. Then the two side walls of the cabin collapsed, and for several minutes the heat was so terrific that he had to back away.

After that, the fire died quickly, there being little left to burn. Soon there was only a pile of glowing embers. Don decided it would be safe to tie the horse. He looped the reins around a bush, and approached the ruins on foot.

His first faint glimmer of hope came when he discovered that there was only one dead horse in the burned-out corral. It was impossible to tell which one it was, Red's pinto or Sammy's bay, but if one of them had been gone when the fire started, perhaps Red ...

A gun barked, the bullet sending up a puff of ashes at

Don's feet. On the heels of the shot, a voice cried fiercely, "That one missed on purpose. Don't move, or by God . . ."

"Red!" Don yelled. "It's me. Don't shoot." He stood motionless, praying that the boy wouldn't get buck fever as he had a few nights before. When ten seconds had passed without another shot, he raised his hands and turned slowly toward the source of the shot. "Hold your fire, Red."

Red Marlowe stepped out from behind a tree, his rifle aimed at Don's chest. He moved stiffly toward the burned cabin, his face contorted with either rage or shock. Finally, he let out his breath in a loud groan, and lowered the rifle.

"So it's really you. I thought at first it was a trick. The horse that's tied over there . . ."

"I borrowed it," Don explained. He moved over and grabbed Red's shoulders. "My God, boy, I thought you were in the cabin."

"I would've been, except for luck. That fool pinto of mine evidently ain't ever been penned up with another horse. He got to raising such a ruckus that I decided the best thing would be to keep 'em apart. While I was away from the cabin, they set it on fire." He looked at Don uncertainly. "Maybe if I'd stayed inside like you told me to, they wouldn't have . . ."

"Don't worry about that now. Chances are they could have burned it regardless. Just be thankful you're alive. Now tell me the rest of it. Who did it?"

"It was them bastards from Box C," Don said grimly. "Whitey Larson and some of his crew."

Don looked at him in surprise.

"You're sure it was Larson? How long ago did it happen?"

"Two, three hours. Hell, I don't know. It was Larson, all right, though; I got a good look at that white hair of his. Why?"

"Nothing," Don said, unable to account for a vague feeling of disappointment. Larson hadn't struck him as the kind of person to burn a man's cabin. Still, the Box C foreman had warned him not to count on anything. And the time fitted all right. Larson and his three men could have burned the cabin, and then reached town by the time

Don had seen them. "Let's have the rest of it, Red. Did you follow them?"

Red shook his head.

"I didn't dare move until they rode out. Then, by the time I got my horse, they was too far away." He looked up at Don and grinned. "I did something better, though; I rode over to Box C and set fire to Culver's big hay barn."

"You set fire to . . . ?"

"What's the matter?" Red asked uneasily. "Didn't you want me to?"

"You did all right, I guess," Don said. "If they want war, I said we'd give it to them. I reckon this is it. Where's your horse?"

"Over there," Red said, pointing.

"Well, go get him. We're not going to win this war by standing here talking."

"You mean we're going over to Box C?"

"The sooner the better. Losing one barn won't hurt Culver too much, but maybe if we hit before Larson and the others get back from town, we'll have a chance at something else."

"Yes sir!" Red said joyfully. "We might even set fire to the house, and plug old man Culver when he tries to get out. That's what would settle this business for good—a bullet right between the old bastard's eyes."

"Now hold on," Don said, but Red was already running for his horse, and Don let him go. Probably the boy was right; now that it had started, it wouldn't stop until someone was dead. He looked around at the ashes and tightened his lips. As far as Culver knew, someone might be dead already. In fact, someone was—Sammy Harding.

Red rode back into the clearing as Don swung into his own saddle. He had intended to turn the borrowed horse loose and let it find its way home, but, now that Sammy's bay was dead, he'd have to hang onto it a while longer. He refused to think of it as stolen, although he was sure that that was what the sheriff would call it. Well, before this night was over, horse-stealing might be one of his lesser crimes.

Red was riding bareback, but fortunately he had bridled the pinto before taking it out to picket. He waited for Don to come up beside him, and said curiously, "I ain't seen the Kelso Kid since he rode out. Did he show up in town?"

"Not where I could see him, anyway," Don said. "Now remember, Red, we're not an Indian raiding-party. Maybe we'll burn the house, but if we do, we'll make sure there's no women in it. The first thing is to get there without being stopped." He looked at Red thoughtfully. "You know, I've never seen this Box C headquarters. Can you tell me anything about it?"

"Not much, I reckon. Of course I had a look at it tonight, but the only time I ever saw it in daylight was once when I stopped there looking for a job. That was before I came to work for Sammy. I can tell you this much: there's the biggest damned house you ever saw, a bunkhouse, a cookshack, and a lot of sheds and things. Also a horsebarn and corral, and"— he grinned—"a pile of ashes where the haybarn was. The whole shebang lies in a little hollow. Does that help any?"

"It might," Don said. "Let's ride." He gigged his horse, and headed it toward the creek, Red's following close behind.

CHAPTER FIFTEEN

WHEN HELEN WAS still a mile short of Culver's headquarters, she noticed a pale glow in the sky. It became brighter with each passing moment, and presently she saw sparks rising. Minutes later, a horse came thundering from the direction of Box C. It slid to a stop before reaching her, and she was startled to hear Claire Culver's voice call out anxiously, "Who is it?"

"Helen Sprecher," Helen answered quickly, pulling up in the middle of the road. "What in the world are you up to?" Claire exclaimed in surprise, and spurred her mount into

a lunging gallop. Without slowing down, she called out in
passing, "Someone set fire to pa's haybarn. I'm going after
Whitey Larson and . . ." Her voice trailed off in the distance.

Helen watched until Claire was out of sight, then went
on toward Box C, her troubled eyes on the glow of the fire.
Already it was beginning to fade, but she knew that the
results would linger after the last ember was dead.

Her first thought was that Don Harding had started it.
He seemed the logical suspect, considering the treatment he
and his brother had received at the hands of Culver and
those who took Culver's orders. Then it occurred to her that
in order for Don to have started the fire, he would have
had to move with almost unbelievable speed. It hadn't been
more than fifteen minutes from the time he had gone into
Ruby Salmon's place until Helen had ridden out of town.
With only that much of a start, and maybe less if he hadn't
found a horse immediately, he would have had to reach Box
C, set fire to the barn, and still have left enough time for
Claire to get a good start toward town.

It was possible, but not probable. For some reason, this
improbability relieved her mind. She didn't like to think of
Don as an arsonist, no matter what his provocation. Still,
if he hadn't done it, who had? Was it someone who hated
him and wanted to incite Cletus Culver to violence?

She came within sight of the buildings, and, by then, there
was nothing left of the haybarn except a bed of smoldering
embers. Three men were standing nearby with water-buckets
in their hands, apparently ready to extinguish any sparks
which might fall on one of the other, buildings. One of the
three turned his head, saw Helen in the light of the rising
moon, and called, "Who's there?"

Helen identified herself, and walked her horse over beside
him, while he and the other two men watched with sus-
picion.

"What the thunder are you doing out here?" Culver demanded. "If you're looking for Harding, he's been here and
gone."

"What makes you think I'd be looking for him?" Helen
asked coolly. "And even if I were, why would I look, out
here? Especially when I saw him in town just before I left."

"How *long* before you left? What is this, anyway, some

smart scheme of Harding's to make it look like he ain't the one that set fire to the haybarn?"

"Mr. Harding doesn't even know I'm here. As for your other question, I saw him in town just ten or fifteen minutes before I rode out." She motioned toward the ashes. "How long ago did this start, Mr. Culver?"

"Not long," Culver said shortly. "Not so long but that Harding could've got here in time to start it after you saw him—if you really did see him." He scowled at her in the moonlight. "If it ain't on account of him, what are you here for?"

"I want to talk to Minnie."

"Minnie!" Culver threw a quick glance toward the house. "You mean to say you rode out here in the middle of the night for a fool thing like that? What do you want to see Minnie about?"

Lying didn't come naturally to Helen, so she said, without any attempt at subterfuge, "I want her to tell me the truth about how she got into the condition she's in."

"Why damn it!" Culver flared. "Everybody already knows. That good-for-nothing Harding kid . . ." He broke off, and said sullenly, "I've got no time to waste on nonsense like this. Besides, Minnie's asleep. Doc White gave her something . . ."

"Can you call it nonsense when it's liable to end up with more folks being killed? maybe you yourself? Let me talk to her, Mr. Culver. Maybe I can . . ."

"You're crazy," Culver snorted. "If she had anything else to say, don't you suppose she'd say it to her own pa?"

"There's some things she'd feel freer to talk about with another woman," Helen said, controlling her temper with difficulty.

"She's got a sister, if she wants a woman to talk to. Anyway, we ain't going to stand here arguing about it. Just turn that horse and go back to town. You've got no call messing in my business anyhow."

Helen clamped her lips to keep from blurting out something she would be sure to regret later. After all, Culver was within his rights. Within his legal rights, at least, which would be all that mattered to him. This was his property, and Minnie was his daughter. Helen threw a frustrated look at the house, reined the horse around, and rode out of the yard, not looking back until she was hidden by a bend in the road.

At this point, she drew the horse to a stand, and got out of the saddle. Maybe Culver had a right to order her to leave, but other folks had rights, too; for instance, the right to know the truth if it would save human lives. Besides, she'd be darned if she was going to go to the trouble of stealing a horse and coming this far, only to be bullied into riding meekly back to town. She led the horse some distance off the road, tied it to a low bush, and circled back toward the house on foot.

When Don reached the ridge which divided Box C from his own land, he waited for Red to come up beside him.

"You'd better take the lead from here on; you know this country better than I do. But remember, Culver may be doing the same thing we are, and we don't want to bump into him in the dark."

"Don't worry," Red said confidently. "I'll steer clear of the regular trail. And if we do run into 'em . . ." He raised his rifle suggestively.

"Take it easy with that gun," Don warned. "This is pretty sure to end up in gunplay before it's over, but I'd rather no one could say we fired the first shot."

"Sure," Red said lightly. "But when it does come to shooting, I mean to put a bullet in Cletus Culver."

Don didn't answer, except to motion for Red to lead off. He was reminded of something the Kelso Kid had said, about Red being like a horse which hadn't been properly broken, that he would likely start to buck when things got tight. Judging from the way he was getting his mind set on killing Cletus Culver, it was beginning to look as though the Kelso Kid might have been right. However, it was too late to do anything about it now.

They had ridden perhaps another mile, when Red stopped his horse and pointed to one side.

"Right about here's where I lost the trail of them cows of yours. Wouldn't you say they was being driven toward Culver's layout?"

Don nodded, and waved him on. His own anger against

Culver was beginning to build. Three cows, or three dozen for that matter, would mean nothing to the owner of Box C. Stealing them had been an obvious attempt at harassment.

Red didn't stop again until they came to a little motte of trees. He waited for Don to pull alongside, then said in a low voice, "It's right over the next rise. Smell that burned hay?"

The smell had been noticeable for some time, and was now quite strong. It wasn't an unpleasant odor, except to the man who owned the hay. Not like the putrid smell of burned horseflesh. Don's lips thinned at the recollection of what Culver's men had done to Sammy's bay, and he reached over to hand his reins to Red.

"You stay right here for the time being. I'm going to take a look over the hill and see what we're up against." He dismounted, and approached the little rise, ducking low so as not to outline himself against the sky. Before he reached the hump, he dropped to the ground and squirmed along on his belly.

From the rim, he could look down into the Box C yard, perhaps a quarter of a mile away. Lights showed in some of the windows of the big house, and from a lantern at the door of what appeared to be a horsebarn. As Don watched, two men came out of the barn. One of them paused beneath the lantern to take off his hat and rub a sleeve across his forehead. Don saw that it was Whitey Larson.

The front door of the house opened, and a man stepped off the veranda and hurried toward the barn, his stocky build and quick, nervous motions marking him as Cletus Culver. He gestured to Whitey Larson and said something which Don couldn't make out. However, his meaning became evident when Larson entered the barn and came out moments later riding a horse and leading another. Larson's voice rose in a shout, and most of the men in the yard swung up to their saddles, Culver mounting the horse brought by his foreman.

Again Culver said something, his hat bobbing in the moonlight. At this, Larson pointed to two of the mounted men, wheeled his horse on its haunches, and headed east, followed by the two men he had designated. At the same time, Culver and two other riders took off down the road toward town. This left two more Box C men in the yard, apparently assigned to guard the buildings.

Don heard a noise beside him, and saw that Red had defied orders by leaving the horses and crawling up to find out what was going on. He was sliding the rifle along in front of him. As he saw what was happening down below, he muttered a curse and threw the rifle to his shoulder, swinging the muzzle toward the three men headed toward town. Before he could pull the trigger, Don reached out and clamped a hand over the hammer.

"Don't be a fool, boy! Shoot that rifle now, and we're dead. They've got us boxed on three sides."

Red whirled on him fiercely, his eyes gleaming in the yellow light.

"Damn it, if you'd've let me alone, I could've got Culver."

"That wouldn't've been a lot of consolation to us when they put the ropes around our necks," Don said shortly. "If you can't follow orders, just say so. You're free to draw your pay and leave any time you want to."

The boy's shoulders sagged, and he said with resentment, "All right. I'll do what you say, but before this is over you're going to wish you'd let me plug the bastard."

"That's a chance I'll have to take. I'm not going to start shooting people from ambush. I've already told you why."

"Then what *are* we going to do, just sit on our butts?"

Don let go of Red's rifle, and edged back from the ridge. The noise made by the departing riders had dwindled, and there was a chance that the sound of voices might carry to the men in the yard. He backed off to where Red had left the horses, and waited for the boy to join him.

"I came over here with the idea we might teach Culver a few tricks about starting fires, but now that he and most of his men have ridden out, I've got a better idea. Something I've been wanting to do from the start. This may be my chance to talk to that girl."

"To Minnie?" Red exploded. "What good will that do? She'll just tell you the same thing she told her pa and Doc White."

"So I've been led to believe," Don said dryly, "But there

are some things I like to find out for myself. If you don't
feel like going along with it, just say so."

Red was quiet a moment, then said resignedly, "All right,
you're still the boss." He gave Don an uncertain grin. "I'm
sorry if I forgot it for a second."

"No harm done, Red; just don't forget it again. Now the
first thing we have to do is get past those two men in the
yard. We'll leave the horses here and try sneaking up on
foot."

"What if someone spots us from the house, say one of
the Culver girls?"

"If they do, we're in trouble. Chances are, though, they'll
be looking toward H Bar H if they're looking at all. That's
the direction they'll be expecting trouble to come from.
Which means we'll have to move in from the other side.
Come on." He stepped out rapidly to the north, keeping
below the little hump. When he felt that they were far
enough above the ranch yard for it to be safe, he turned
west, making a wide circle so as to approach the house from
the back.

Red moved along beside him, saying nothing, but somehow managing to convey the impression that he was doing
this under protest. This didn't add to Don's peace of mind.
He wished now that he had taken the Kelso Kid's advice
and let the boy go. Now it was too late, for Red seemed to
have developed such a mania for killing Culver that he was
sure to try sooner or later. Better to have him here, where
he could be controlled to some extent, than roaming around
on his own.

They reached a point some distance west of the yard,
and stopped beneath a solitary cottonwood to survey the
house, this side of which lay in its own shadow. Light glowed
faintly through the curtains of two adjacent windows; other
than this, there was no break in the darkness.

Don put his lips close to Red's ear, and said softly, "One
of us will make less noise than two, so I'm going down there
alone. I want you to stay right here under this tree unless
I run into trouble. Can I count on you for that?"

"I'll stay," Red promised. "But if you get in a jam ..."

"If I do, you'll know it," Don said grimly. "In that case,
come a-shooting." Without waiting for Red to ask any more

questions, he left the cottonwood and ran swiftly to the shelter of a small shed. When nothing happened, he bent low and moved across a patch of moonlight into the shadow of the building.

Now that he was in darkness himself, he could make out more details of the house, including its seven or eight dark windows, and the two which were dimly lighted. He felt his way carefully to the back wall, dropped to his knees so as to pass beneath the windowsills, and crept cautiously toward the north end.

There was a narrow strip of shadow along the north side, just wide enough so that he could risk looking around the corner. He did, and saw one of the two guards leaning against a corner post of the veranda, smoking a cigarette. The man's back was turned, and he seemed to be staring off toward the east.

Don drew his pistol, eased around the corner of the house, and inched his way forward, hugging the shade next to the building. He had almost reached the veranda when a twig snapped under his boot. The guard whirled, grabbing for his gun. Before he could call out, Don hit him over the head with the pistol. The man sighed softly, and Don caught him as he fell, easing him to the ground close to the house.

The next few seconds seemed an eternity, but nothing broke the silence. Don removed the man's belt, and used it to strap his ankles together. He found a bandana in the guard's pocket, twisted it into a roll, and bound his wrists behind his back. Don's own neckerchief served as a gag.

There was a railing across the end of the veranda. Don slid under it, and moved along the front of the house toward the door. He paused there long enough to locate the other guard at the far end of the veranda, his cigarette glowing in the darkness. When the glow disappeared as the man turned his head, Don tried the door, found it unlocked, and eased it open. He entered the house, and closed the door carefully behind him.

The room he was in appeared to be a hallway. From where he stood, he could see that the lighted room on his left was a big parlor. At its far end, a door presumably led to the rooms beyond. Closer at hand, a second door on the right opened out of the hallway to the rooms of the north end of the house. Rather than risk crossing the lighted parlor, Don elected to investigate this other section of the house first. He turned the knob carefully, and put a little weight on the door.

The room it opened into was almost completely dark, and smelled strongly of cooking. Don slid through the doorway, waited until his eyes became adjusted to the darkness, and then was able to make out the shape of a large oblong table. Evidently this was the dining room, and, from the smell, the kitchen would be just beyond. He returned to the hall.

There was no way to avoid crossing the lighted parlor now. He took a deep breath and walked rapidly toward the door at the far end, thankful for the rugs which deadened the sound of his boots. When he reached the comparative safety of the dark doorway beyond, he let out his breath in relief.

There was still no way of telling which room was Minnie's. Presumably Claire was sleeping somewhere in the house, or more likely, was awake, in view of the hulabaloo shortly before. If he should be unlucky enough to blunder into her room instead of her sister's ...

For the moment, however, he seemed to be in no great danger. The hallway he had just entered extended to the south end of the house, where a window threw back faint reflections of the lighted parlor. Along each side of the hall were closed doors, three on the left, and two on the right.

Don tried to figure some way of determining which room would be Minnie's. He decided to eliminate those on the side with only two doors. Since they would be larger rooms, it seemed likely that one of them would be Culver's. Probably the other was kept for guests. If not, if it was used by one of the girls, Don had an idea Claire would be the one. From what he had seen of her, she wouldn't be satisfied with a room smaller than her sister's.

This narrowed the choice to the three on the left side. Since there was no way of guessing which was Minnie's, he decided to take a chance on the last in the row, which at least would have the advantage of putting him farther from the front door. In case Culver should return unexpectedly, there might be a chance of getting out through a window.

He reached the last door on the left, and it opened easily under his touch. As he stepped inside, he knew that he was at least partly right in his reasoning. Only a room used by a woman would smell so sweetly of cologne. He closed the door quietly and stood listening. Somewhere in the room someone breathed softly as though in sleep. He moved toward the sound, and the pale moonlight from a window in the south wall disclosed the dim bulk of a bed. He took another step, intending to cover the girl's mouth with his hand to prevent her crying out. As he stretched out his arm, a noise behind him made him jerk his head around. He had a fleeting glimpse of a dim figure with upraised arms. Then something hit the top of his skull, and everything went black.

CHAPTER SIXTEEN

CULVER WAS IN an ugly mood when he started toward town. The two men riding with him recognized this, and knew him well enough to keep quiet. However, he had his own bitter thoughts for company, and, by the time he reached Paradise, his disposition was worse than before. It wasn't helped any when he pulled up in front of the sheriff's office, and saw Yankton slumped in a chair behind his desk.

Yankton looked up as Culver jerked open the door and came in. Before he could collect his wits, Culver said scathingly, "I take it you've got Harding back there in a cell. Right?"

The sheriff stared at him stupidly, turned to look toward the cells, and said with obvious lack of comprehension, "Harding? No, sir, he ain't here. He got away."

"Then why the hell ain't you out looking for him?" Culver thundered, and went on to answer his own question. "I'll tell you why; you're afraid you might find him."

"Now hold on, Mr. Culver," Yankton protested. "You've got no call to say that. I've been looking for him until an hour ago. I'm just waiting now for daylight so I can pick up his trail."

"Sure, and while you're waiting here on your big fat butt, he's out setting fire to my haybarn. By God, Yankton, when I made you sheriff, I must've been out of my mind. The first time a real man shows up, he makes you look like a greenhorn. First you try to outdraw him, and he knocks the gun out of your hand. Then you go after him with a scattergun, and what happens? He plugs that knothead you pretended to deputize, and bends a pistol over your head."

Yankton's face flushed, and he said uneasily, "Who told you about that?"

"It don't matter who told me. Everybody in town knows it by now." Culver reached across the desk, grabbed the sheriff's shirt, and hauled him to his feet. "Go out and find him, you fool, before he does something else."

"Yes, sir," Yankton mumbled, looking as though he were relieved that it hadn't turned out even more disastrously. "I'll find him, all right, and when I do . . ." He glanced out the door at the two Box C riders, and lowered his voice. "When I do, do you want him taken care of like we did his . . . ?"

"Shut up!" Culver said contemptuously. "You really are a fool, ain't you? Do you actually think we could pull the same trick twice? This ain't a green kid we're talking about now, and he ain't been fooling around with a girl. Besides, the folks in this town are more scared of him now than they are of you. If you ever expect to carry any more weight around here, you'd better take care of him yourself."

"I aim to," the sheriff boasted. "Don't you worry about that, Mr. Culver."

"It ain't my worry, Yankton. It's yours." Culver frowned. "How did he slip through your fingers the last time?"

"He stole a horse over at Ruby Salmon's."

"Then that's your grounds for bringing him in. Now get moving."

"Yes sir," Yankton said again, and looked at Culver inquisitively. "Where'll you be, in case I have something to report?"

"I'm going back to the ranch. There's just two of my men watching the place, and the way Harding works, that might not be enough." Culver stomped out of the room, flung himself into his saddle, then yelled back through the doorway, "Where's Claire? The last I saw of her, she was leaving for town to tell Larson about the fire."

"Here I am, Pa," Claire said, and Culver saw that she had ridden up while he had been in the sheriff's office. "From the way you've been shouting, I take it you haven't found Don Harding."

"No, but I will," Culver growled. "Just give me time."

"Oh, you'll find him, all right. The only thing is, you're liable to find him looking at you along a gunbarrel."

Culver yanked savagely on his reins, whirled the horse around, and sank spurs into its flanks. It took off wildly toward Box C, the other two men having to lash their mounts to keep up. From behind came the sound of Claire's laughter, then the pound of her horse's hoofs as she brought up the rear.

Ten minutes later, Sheriff Yankton rode out from behind the office and took off toward H Bar H. He was still seething from the tongue lashing given him by Culver. You did a man's dirty work for him for years, then when something went a little bit wrong, he lit on your with both feet. If that damned Harding hadn't showed up ...

By the time Yankton reached the H Bar H turn off, he had convinced himself that all his troubles were Don Harding's fault. The next time they met, he promised himself, he'd kill the bastard, even if it meant shooting him in the back. If that didn't shut Culver up, maybe there was another bullet with Culver's name on it.

Don Harding opened his eyes and saw Helen Sprecher leaning over him, her eyes regarding him anxiously. He made an effort to sit up, but she placed a hand on his chest and held him down.

"Lie still for a minute, Mr. Harding. You've been un-

conscious for half an hour; that was a hard blow you took."
Don was too groggy to do anything but follow orders. He
rolled his eyes, and saw that he was still in the bedroom,
and that someone, presumably Helen, had lit a lamp. As
his head began to clear and memory returned, he again tried
to sit up, and this time Helen made no effort to stop him.
After a momentary spasm of dizziness, he focused his eyes
on her.

"Who hit me? and where'd he go?"

"I hit you, Mr. Harding. I was . . ."

"You? Why in the name of common sense . . . ?"

"Now don't fly off the handle," Helen said. "And keep
your voice down. There may be somebody within hearing
distance."

"I'm sorry. I guess I'm just not used to being clobbered
by a woman."

"Maybe you're not in the habit of breaking into women's
bedrooms. If I'd been able to see who you were, I wouldn't
have hit you."

"That's a comforting thought," Don said. He dragged
himself to his feet, and looked down at the bed. To his
surprise, the girl was still sleeping. He turned a puzzled
glance toward Helen.

"Is that Minnie Culver?"

Helen nodded, and went on to explain. "She's been sleeping like this ever since I got here. From what her father
said, Doc White gave her something to let her sleep. I'm
waiting to talk to her when she wakes up."

"You mean Culver let you . . . ?"

"Mr. Culver doesn't even know I'm here," Helen said,
smiling crookedly. "In fact, he ordered me off the place. I
came back and found a window open, but that's all the good
it's done me so far. Minnie didn't even wake up when I
knocked you out."

"When she does, what're you planning to talk to her
about?"

"I'm going to try to persuade her to tell me the truth
about what happened to her." Helen looked at him speculatively. "Is that why you're here, too?"

Don nodded without answering. He was trying to figure

out Helen Sprecher. One minute she was a rather prim
proprietor of a restaurant, professing to detest violence. The
next, she was breaking into a house after being ordered to
stay away, and looking like a roughneck—a very pretty
roughneck, incidentally. What was it the Kelso Kid had
said about not judging women or horses by their rigging?

"Well, is it?" Helen repeated. "Because if it is, there's
no sense in my staying around. It won't take two of us to
hear what she has to say."

"No, but I've got an idea she'd come nearer telling the
truth to you, if you don't mind waiting. Besides, I've got
other things to take care of."

"Other things?"

"That's right. For one, there's a guard out in the yard
that may find his partner where I left him tied. If he does,
he's liable to start raising a fuss. Then there's Culver and
his crew to think about. They hightailed it out of here a
while ago, probably looking for me, but they're liable to
come back any minute. Another thing, Red Marlowe's
waiting for me to show up, and Red isn't famous for being
patient. I'm surprised he hasn't busted loose already." He
gave Helen a level look.

"Will you do me a favor, miss? And wait to talk to the
girl?"

"I'll do it," she promised, "as a favor to Sammy." She
frowned. "Tell me, Mr. Harding, what did you hope to
accomplish by burning Mr. Culver's haybarn?"

"Nothing. To tell the truth, I didn't burn it. But Red
Marlowe did, and I don't know as I blame him, considering
that he had to watch some of Culver's men burn our cabin,
and Sammy's horse along with it. Not to mention that
they shot Red in the leg a little earlier."

"Mr. Culver did that?" Helen asked in astonishment.

"His men did, and that's the same thing. Just like I'm
responsible for what happened to his haybarn." Don stooped
for his hat, which had rolled under the edge of the bed.
"One more thing, how can I get out of here without bump-
ing into this girl's sister?"

"Claire isn't here," Helen said. "She rode into town to
tell Whitey Larson about the fire, and hasn't come back.

In fact, there's nobody in this end of the house except us."
She shook her head glumly. "I don't understand it. Mr.
Culver's barn and your cabin have been destroyed, and,
according to what you just told me, there's been a horse
burned to death, and yet nothing's been settled. Where
does it all end?"

"I wish I knew," Don said soberly. "But unless I get
moving, it's liable to end for me right here." He grinned.
"Next time we meet, I hope you recognize me before you
start swinging." He crossed to the door and let himself
out into the hall.

Now that he knew there were no occupants in the other
rooms at this end of the house, it seemed safe enough to
leave through one of the windows. He entered one of the
big bedrooms across the hall, found a window open, and let
himself out into the shadow, which was now considerably
narrower than before. Without stopping to close the window,
he started off toward the place where he had left Red.

He had just barely reached the edge of the shadow, when
a voice behind him said, harshly, "Just hold it that way,
mister. You make a hell of a good target where you are."

Don froze, but still might have made a try for his gun,
except that another voice said from a different direction, "Go
ahead and reach for it, Harding. I'll be glad of an excuse
to square things for the wallop you gave me."

With two of them against him, and neither in sight, the
odds were hopeless. Don raised his hands at his sides,
and stood waiting. Boots crunched the gravel behind him,
and he felt his gun being lifted from his holster. Then
something hard was jabbed into his back, and the first
voice said, "Get out in the middle of the yard, mister, and
don't try anything. My partner don't like you very much
as it is."

"I'll say I don't," the other man said. "For two cents,
I'd let him have it right here."

"Take it easy, Ollie; the boss likely wants to talk to
him first."

The one called Ollie merely grunted, and the other one
prodded Don in the ribs. "Get going, mister."

They reached the moonlit space near the burned barn,

and Don was ordered to stop, while the two guards took up positions from which they could keep him covered. Don glanced toward the house, wondering if Helen was aware of what was going on. Not that it would make much difference. She had demonstrated unexpected qualities tonight, but even if she had a gun, which he doubted, and knew how to use it, she would be impotent against two armed men.

Red seemed the better bet, and if he had remained under the cottonwood, according to instructions, he should have been able to see Don taken prisoner, but there still was no sign of him.

Before Don could give it much thought, the rumble of hoofs gave warning of the approach of riders. They pounded into the yard, and Don saw that it was Cletus Culver himself who was in the lead, followed by two of his men, and, at a greater distance, by Claire. The three men pulled their mounts to a stop, and Culver let out a triumphant shout.

"Harding, by God! Where'd you catch him?"

"Coming out of your house, Mr. Culver. He was sneaking . . ."

"Out of my house!" Culver whirled in his saddle, and pointed a pistol at Don's belly. "What were you looking for in there, Harding? If you've done anything to . . ."

"I didn't touch Minnie, if that's what you're getting at," Don said. "I wanted to talk to her, but she wouldn't . . ."

"Don't let him fool you, Mr. Culver," one of the guards said. "She talked, all right. We heard her. Couldn't make out what they were saying, but it was a woman's voice part of the time."

Don's breath caught in his throat. If Culver should find Helen in Minnie's bedroom . . . He lifted his shoulders in a shrug.

"All right, so they heard her. What I meant was that she wouldn't tell me anything new. She still claims it was Sammy."

"Sure, because that's who it was," Culver said, with satisfaction. "But it wasn't Sammy that burned my barn, and that's what we're concerned with now. I suppose you'll deny that, too?"

Don was silent a moment, then shook his head. It wasn't

going to make any difference to Culver whose hand had actually scratched the match, so why drag Red into it? Maybe the boy would see what was going on, and be smart enough to get away.

"Your barn was all right until after you had Larson burn my cabin, Culver."

Culver's head jerked up.

"What the hell're you talking about? I didn't have . . ."

"Then Larson did it on his own, but he knew it was what you wanted."

"Maybe he did," Culver said. "Anyway, it don't make much difference now. I warned you that first day to get out of the country, but you was too damned smart. Now you're in for it. You've not only burned my barn, but you shot a deputy, knocked out the sheriff, and stole a horse." His lips drew back in a grin. "Maybe you're smart, mister, but you ain't smart enough to get out of this." He motioned to one of his men.

"Get him a horse, Kramer; we'll take him to the sheriff."

The man called Kramer rode off toward the horse barn, while the other four remained in a loose ring around their prisoner. Don waited quietly, knowing it would be senseless to try to escape now. His own situation was hopeless, at least for the present, but there was some satisfaction in the knowledge that at least he had diverted attention from the house. With any luck at all, Helen should be able to get away. For some reason, this seemed vitally important to him.

Kramer was just leading a spare horse out of the barn when Claire said unexpectedly, "Pa, I think . . ."

"Never mind what you think," Culver snapped. "You've caused enough trouble as it is, so just shut up."

"Don't talk to me as if I were one of your hired hands," Claire said furiously. "Besides, all I wanted to say was that I think I hear riders coming. Maybe the sheriff's going to save you a ride."

By then they could all hear it. A moment later, five horsemen came into sight from the direction of H Bar H. They paused a moment on top of the ridge, then headed down into the hollow.

CHAPTER SEVENTEEN

ALTHOUGH IT NO longer seemed to make much difference, Don wondered idly who the riders would turn out to be. Three of them were probably Whitey Larson and his two Box C hands. Perhaps the fourth, as Claire had suggested, would be Sheriff Yankton. But the fifth . . . ?

They pounded into the yard, and Don saw that the fifth was the Kelso Kid, looking as unconcerned as ever. The others were Sheriff Yankton and the three Box C men. Yankton almost rode Don down before jerking his horse to a stop. He drew his pistol, but before he could bring it into line, the Kelso Kid said mildly, "Hold it a minute, Sheriff. Let's hear what this feller has to say for himself."

It was enough to distract the sheriff momentarily, but not to make him holster his gun. He turned in the saddle, and saw the Kelso Kid sitting quietly with his hands crossed on the horn of his saddle. There was nothing threatening in the Kelso Kid's attitude, yet the sheriff hesitated.

"What's it to you what he has to say?"

"Just curious, I reckon," the Kelso Kid said. "Or maybe it's because you're pointing a gun at him when he ain't even got so much as a gravel shooter. The way it looks to me, he ain't going to have much chance no matter what he says, so why not let him talk?"

For the moment, the affair had narrowed to an argument between Yankton and the Kelso Kid. Even Culver was silent as he waited for the outcome. However, Don knew that nothing the Kelso Kid could say would affect the outcome, so he said, "Thanks for trying, Kelso, but it's no use. This deck was stacked before you showed up."

"About what I figured, Harding, and I've been going up

138

against stacked decks long enough to recognize one. Sort of gets to be a habit."

Don noticed now that the Kelso Kid had stopped his horse in a spot which put no one in back of him. Apparently the others had made the same discovery, for none of them showed any inclination to take sides. Whitey Larson was smiling as though he were secretly enjoying the by-play.

It was Culver who broke the silence by turning to Larson and saying irritably, "Who the hell is this feller? And what's he doing here anyway?"

"Calls himself the Kelso Kid, Mr. Culver. He was over at Harding's place. Seems like somebody burned the cabin, and this feller was poking around in the ashes to see if anyone got caught inside."

Don swung his eyes toward Larson, wishing it were light enough to see the man's expression. What he had just said seemed strange for a man who had himself set fire to the cabin, unless of course Larson was just a good actor. But if Larson had started the fire, why would he bother to pretend now that he hadn't?

Culver's voice interrupted Don's thoughts.

"You, Kelso, or whatever your name is, what's your interest in this?"

"My interest? Hell, I've got no interest. Like I just told the sheriff, I'm curious about what Harding has to say. For that matter, I've always wondered what that brother of his said before they strung him up. Nobody that was there seems to want to talk about it."

Don didn't think the Kelso Kid would do so much talking without a good reason. Perhaps he was just attracting attention to himself to give Don a chance to do something. Don looked at the men nearest him, and saw they were no longer watching him.

"Another thing," the Kelso Kid said, and now Don was sure that he was up to something. "This tinhorn sheriff you've got couldn't . . ."

Don lunged at the closest rider, clawing for the man's holstered gun. His fingers closed around the grips and he jerked it free, whirling to face the sheriff, whose sixgun was just coming into line. Both guns went off at the same time. A horse behind Don squealed in pain and surprise, and began to buck. Sheriff Yankton toppled out of the saddle, his gun clattering on the ground.

All the horses were plunging, making accurate shooting impossible, and giving Don a temporary advantage. He leveled his gun at Culver, and yelled, "Tell them to hold their fire, or you get the same as the sheriff!"

Before Culver could answer, a gun sounded from some distance away, and a woman screamed; the sound seemed to come from inside the house. Don's first thought was of Helen. Forgetting his own danger, he whirled and ran toward the house. As he did, the gun spoke again, and Culver let out a surprised gasp.

Don was vaguely aware of others behind him as he burst into the house and raced across the parlor. He reached Minnie's room and opened the door.

Slumped on the floor beside the bed was Minnie Culver, blood staining the front of her nightgown. Helen Sprecher was bending over her, trying to stem the flow with her bare hand. She looked up despairingly as Don entered, then moved aside to let him pick Minnie up and lay her gently on the bed. By then, others had reached the room. Without looking at them, Don said sharply, "Somebody go for the doctor. Hurry!"

"One of the boys already left," Whitey Larson said. "Mr. Culver's in bad shape, too. Whoever did this put a slug in him. I'm afraid he's a goner."

As he finished speaking, Claire Culver pushed past him, her face ashen. She saw her sister on the bed, crossed the room stiffly, and brushed Don and Helen out of the way.

"I'll take care of her. God knows I've waited long enough. Somebody get some water from the kitchen."

Larson nodded to one of the men, and he ran out of the room, although it was fairly evident from the amount of blood that Minnie was beyond help.

Don took Helen's arm and led her gently across the room to a chair.

"What happened? Did you see who did it?"

Helen shook her head woodenly. "It was someone outside the window. Whoever it was must have been listening. When Minnie finally agreed to tell the truth, he shot her."

"Good God! She might . . ."

Helen placed her fingers against his lips, and nodded toward the bed. He turned and saw Claire leaning down as though trying to hear something Minnie was saying. After a bit, she straightened up and backed away, her chin trembling. She saw Don watching her, and said in a faint voice, "It wasn't your brother at all. That time Red Marlowe came out here looking for a job, she and he . . ." Her voice trailed off and she began to cry, her shoulders shaken by great sobs. She stumbled blindly toward the door, saw Whitey Larson looking at her with his eyes full of compassion, and buried her head on his chest.

For a moment, there was no sound except her sobs, then she said clearly enough for everyone to hear, "All this just because we Culvers thought we were so much better than anybody else. May God forgive us." After that, she was silent as Whitey Larson put his arm around her and led her out of the room.

Some part of Don's mind had registered the sound of running horses soon after the shots, but he had been too worried about Helen to give it much thought. Now he heard the sound again, this time, that of horses moving slowly. The hoofbeats stopped somewhere close by, and presently the Kelso Kid came into the room. He glanced at the bed, took off his hat, and looked around at Don.

"Is she . . .?"

Don nodded, and the Kelso Kid shook his head somberly. "That makes four of them besides Sammy: her, Culver, the sheriff, and Red Marlowe." He sighed. "Damn fool kid; I didn't trust him from the start."

"Why didn't you tell me?" Don asked quietly.

"Wouldn't've done any good. You was so set on making him another Sammy Harding, you wouldn't've believed me. Besides, there was nothing to tell. Just that I couldn't figure a young feller like him hanging around when there was nothing worth staying for."

"And can you figure it out now?"

"Not for certain. He started shooting before I could ask him, and I had no choice."

"I believe I can," Don said. "It goes back to something you said yourself, about waiting to ask the baby who its father was. Likely Red was afraid it would have red hair,

like his, and if it did, there wouldn't be any place he could
run where Culver wouldn't find him. Until he found out,
he couldn't take a chance on leaving." He turned to one of
the Box C men.

"There's something I have to know. Was it Box C that
burned the cabin?"

"No, sir," the man said. "Maybe we've done some dirty
tricks in our lives, but we never burned any horses. Whitey
would've killed us if we'd wanted to."

"That's what's been bothering me," Don said. "I couldn't
figure Larson for the kind of man who'd kill a horse. Red
must've burned the cabin, so as to have an excuse for burning the haybarn and starting a war. Likely he knew, if it
came to a showdown, Culver would be the first one I'd try
for."

Helen said thoughtfully, "Supposing you're right, why
couldn't Minnie have told her father the truth, instead of
putting the blame on Sammy?"

"Probably because she was afraid that if Red got in a
tight spot, he'd tell her father the truth, that it was her
idea as much as his. Culver couldn't hold it against her if
she got raped, but if he found out she had willingly . . ." He
shook his head, and took hold of Helen's elbow.

"There's nothing more we can do around here, or if there
is, I reckon Whitey Larson will do it better than we could.
Let's go."

Helen allowed him to lead her out of the bedroom, across
the big parlor, and into the yard. Over in the east, the sky
was beginning to brighten with the promise of a new day,
the light making little hummocks of the blanket covered
bodies of Culver and the sheriff. Don skirted them at a distance, shielding them from Helen's sight with his own body.
Still holding onto her arm, he walked slowly toward the
horsebarn, passing the bunkhouse, where several of the Box
C men watched impassively.

At the entrance to the barn, Helen said solemnly, "What
do you intend to do now, Mr. Harding?"

"Well . . ." He looked down at her a moment, noting again
how different she looked with her hair hanging softly instead of in that tight little bun. It came to him that he would
feel the same way about her no matter how she looked.

"Well, miss, I still have a ranch to run. I reckon that'll be enough to keep me busy, what with building a new cabin and one thing or another." He hesitated, then went on cautiously, "Speaking of the new cabin, it strikes me I might as well build a regular house this time, with two or three rooms, and glass windows, and things like that. The sort of place a woman might like the looks of. I was wondering if maybe . . ."

"Yes, Mr. Harding?" Helen seemed to be having trouble keeping a straight face.

"Well, I could use a little advice, and you being a woman, I was wondering . . ."

"If I'd help you with the plans? Why yes, Mr. Harding, I believe that could be arranged. Of course, I won't be able to spare much time. I still have a restaurant to run."

"I know," Don said glumly. "And I suppose as long as you have the cafe . . ." He noticed the way she was looking at him, and had an inspiration. "Of course, if something was to happen to the cafe . . ."

"Yes, Mr. Harding?" There was no question about it this time; her eyes were shining.

"Why, miss, if there's nothing stopping you but the restaurant . . ." He glanced at the ashes of the haybarn. "Well, it just so happens I have another match."

"Why, Mr. . . ."

She didn't get to finish, for Don had seen the look in her eyes, and had decided that there had already been too much time wasted in talk. There'd be plenty of chance for that later on.